P9-CCR-929

PEACE MONTESSORI
2315 LONG RD
NEW HAVEN, IN 46774

F Par
Paratore, Colleen Murtagh
Dreamsleeves

DEMCO

IN PRAISE OF *DREAMSLEEVES*

"Put your dreams on your sleeves, and this book in your heart. Honest and uplifting, *Dreamsleeves* shows that while life isn't perfect, it can get better with imagination, hope and, ultimately, the courage to make a change."
— Jennifer Roy, author of *Cordially Uninvited* and *Yellow Star*

"The courage and capacity to keep dreaming, even in the face of serious family problems, makes Aislinn a heroine we all root for."
— Meg Seinberg-Hughes, librarian

"I was immediately struck by the emotional depth and the great heart of this sensitively portrayed and multi-layered story. *Dreamsleeves* is definitely one of my top picks for the year!"
— Rachel King, Little Book House

"A page turner I couldn't put down. I needed to see if Aislinn's dreams would come true. . . . Isn't that what we all wish for?"
— Debbie Dermady, fifth-grade teacher

"Coleen Murtagh Paratore has given readers a reason to wear their dreams on their sleeves. After reading *Dreamsleeves*, you'll believe in the power of dreams, too."
— Joyce R. Laiosa, librarian

"*Dreamsleeves* is empowering and taught me to believe in my dreams! Filled with suspense, romance, inspiration, and a whole lot of love, I never wanted to put the book down."
— Stefanie, age 15

"Coleen Paratore's finest work yet. While the book is written for young readers, it's meant for dreamers of all ages. Keep a tissue handy, you might shed a tear or two. I did."
— Stanley Hadsell, Market Block Books

"I loved getting to know sweet, unselfish Aislinn, and dreaming that she'd overcome her very real challenges. Readers will cheer as

'A' finds a creative, literary way to make her dreams and those of others become realities."　　— Janice Toomajian, librarian

"This book had me yearning for childhood, for that resilient, impermeable hopefulness. . . ."
　　— Peter Marino, author of *Dough Boy* and
　　Magic and Misery

"In the midst of dealing with adult-sized difficulties in her life, Aislinn, through Coleen's beautiful storytelling, manages to keep the essentials of youth—hope and wonder — alive."
　　— Marisa Geraghty, Barnes & Noble Booksellers

"True-to-life and heartbreaking. I was cheering for Aislinn to get every dream she pins on her sleeve!"
　　— Lisa Lehman, librarian

"This sometimes heart wrenching story is crafted by Paratore with tenderness and wisdom. We never stop hoping and believing that 'A' will surely prevail. Despite her harsh reality, she bubbles and sparkles with the joy of life."
　　— Robert Whiteman, teacher

"Coleen Murtagh Paratore gives readers, both young and old, the inspiration to not only dream big, but to know that anything and everything is possible so long as they have the courage to 'wear their dreams on their sleeves.' "
　　—Jamie L. Gillham, school library media specialist

"I am in love with Coleen's books! The idea of the Dreamsleeves is a great one and I plan to try it out! I think that both boys and girls will want to read this book."　　— Colie, age 12

"Aislinn's genuine voice authentically captures her pressures and her stresses, the period and the setting, and her resistance and resilience."　　— Starr LaTronica, librarian

"In *Dreamsleeves*, readers are treated to another page-turner by today's fairy godmother for the young, author Coleen Murtagh

Paratore, but in this one, they'll find answers to tough, life issues." — Sara Webb Quest, author of *Moving Back to Normal*

"Readers will be cheering for the spunky Aislinn as she navigates her way through the ups and downs of life with her big Irish family, learns about friendship and first love, and deals with life's really tough problems. Readers will hear her voice long after they turn the last page of this poignant and powerful novel." — Gail King, librarian

"Hopeful and uplifting. Aislinn does not sacrifice herself or her dreams, and that's what makes the ending especially satisfying." — Rondi Brower, Blackwood & Brouwer Booksellers Ltd.

Dreamsleeves

COLEEN MURTAGH PARATORE

SCHOLASTIC PRESS • NEW YORK

Copyright © 2012 by Coleen Murtagh Paratore

All rights reserved. Published by Scholastic Press, an imprint of Scholastic
Inc., *Publishers since 1920*. SCHOLASTIC, SCHOLASTIC PRESS, and associated logos
are trademarks and/or registered trademarks of Scholastic Inc.

No part of this publication may be reproduced, stored in a retrieval system,
or transmitted in any form or by any means, electronic, mechanical,
photocopying, recording, or otherwise, without written permission of the
publisher. For information regarding permission, write to Scholastic Inc.,
Attention: Permissions Department, 557 Broadway, New York, NY 10012.

Library of Congress Cataloging-in-Publication Data

Paratore, Coleen, 1958–
Dreamsleeves / by Coleen Murtagh Paratore. — 1st ed.
p. cm.
Summary: During a momentous summer, twelve-year-old Aislinn's dreams
include that her father will stop drinking and give her more freedom, that her
fifth sibling will be born safely, that she will not lose her best friend or her
potential boyfriend, and that she can teach members of her community both to
express their dreams and to help others' dreams come true.
[1. Interpersonal relations—Fiction. 2. Family life—New York (State)—Fiction.
3. Alcoholism—Fiction. 4. Hope—Fiction. 5. Catholics—Fiction. 6. Troy
(N.Y.)—Fiction.] I. Title.
PZ7.P2137Dre 2012
[Fic]—dc22   2011003769

ISBN 978-0-545-31020-8

10 9 8 7 6 5 4 3 2 1   12 13 14 15 16

Printed in the U.S.A.   23
First edition, April 2012

The text type was set in Matt Antique BT.
Book design by Elizabeth B. Parisi

To *you* reading these words right now . . .

listen deeply and draw your dream

up and out of your heart,

and when you are ready to make it real,

wear it on your sleeve and *believe*.

With all best wishes always,

COLEEN MURTAGH PARATORE

OTHER BOOKS BY COLEEN MURTAGH PARATORE
THAT YOU MAY ALSO ENJOY:

THE "WILLA" BOOKS . . .

The Wedding Planner's Daughter

The Cupid Chronicles

Willa by Heart

Forget Me Not

Wish I Might

From Willa, With Love

THE "SUNNY" BOOKS . . .

Sunny Holiday

Sweet and Sunny

OTHER NOVELS . . .

Mack McGinn's Big Win

A Pearl Among Princes

The Funeral Director's Son

Kip Campbell's Gift

PICTURE BOOKS . . .

Catching the Sun

26 Big Things Small Hands Do

How Prudence Proovit Proved the
Truth About Fairy Tales

CHAPTER ONE
Wide-Awake Dreams

The dream is the truth.
— Zora Neale Hurston

My name is Aislinn, old Irish for *dream*.

Funny, for a girl whose name means "dream," I never dreamt a dream I could remember in the morning. Surely, I must have them, everybody does — happy dreams, scary dreams, puzzling ones to try and solve.

I only dream when I am awake, and then I write those dreams down so I won't forget. I have lots of wide-awake dreams, enough to fill a book. Maybe I have so many of them that my brain needs to rest at night.

Just as I'm not good at sleep-dreaming, I'm also bad at recalling things that happened long ago, back when it was just the three of us, Mom, Dad, and me, living in the basement of this, my nana's house. Down in that dark place with the just-one window that didn't open, all I could see were squirrels, grass, and the walking-by shoes of my relatives who lived upstairs. Brown loafers meant "Nana." Black boots, "Papa." Tan boots, "Uncle Mark."

There were also two other people whose shoes I should have seen, tenants of my nana's who lived upstairs from her on the second floor; "the old Polish couple," my parents called them, but they might as well have been "the old Polish ghosts" since I never once saw them, shoes or anything.

Then one day when I was six and my mom was expecting a baby, my nana announced that the old Polish couple had moved and that we could have the top floor if we wanted it.

We did.

Perhaps I have forgotten so much from the past because now I am nearly thirteen and there are seven of us, Mom, Dad, and five kids all trying to fit in three little bedrooms while Dad saves enough money to buy our house in the country, the one with the stream and the apple trees.

Nana still lives on the first floor, alone now. Papa and Uncle Mark are in heaven. The basement is empty.

I keep suggesting to my father that the little ones and I, so cramped up here in this too-small apartment, could play tag or kickball or even ride bikes down in the basement, but my father says, no, "It's not fit for rats."

Maybe another reason I'm bad at recalling is because there's so much going on in my right-now life that my brain has no room to hold the old.

This bothers me; I want to remember. There must have been lots of happy times. But no matter how I search through my own mind album, like Sherlock Holmes with a magnifying glass, just four pictures slip out from the basement days.

Picture one . . . It's summer and my papa and I are having a picnic on a blanket on the lawn. I am two, maybe three. The sandwiches are bologna and cheese on white with mayonnaise, cut in triangles; it's warm and sunny and we're laughing, but then I feel something crawling up my leg, then a bite, then another, and I jump up scratching and crying, and Papa is shouting to Nana, "Come quick, sweet Jesus, the girl's got ants in her pants!"

Nana fixed the problem and there was ice cream or lollipops or both and Papa mimicked how I looked jumping about with the ants in my pants — and I joined in and then Nana, too, and we all danced the "Ants Dance," laughing.

Picture two . . . It's Halloween and the doorbell rings. My mom scoops me up in one arm, the plastic pumpkin filled with candy in the other, and we hurry to answer it. *Oh, no!* Two bank robbers with stockings pulled over their faces are staring in at us.

"Give us all your candy or else," one of the robbers demands, pointing a finger pistol at my mother.

Mom screams and drops the pumpkin, clutching me so tightly I think I will burst.

The bank robbers pull off their stocking masks.

"Trick or treat," they shout, laughing.

It's my nana (my nana!?!) and her best friend "from the old country," Mrs. Casey.

"Now, that was a trick, Maggie, wasn't it?" Nana says to my mom, winking at me, tears streaming down her cheeks, clutching her belly laughing. I laugh, too.

My mother doesn't find this funny at all, though, not one teeny bit.

Picture three . . . It's winter and I'm shivering as my mom lifts me out of the kitchen sink, where she has just given me a bath. There was no tub or shower in the basement. This is my youngest memory. . . . I think I was one. My mother wraps me in a towel and puts me on the sink ledge too close to where an iron is cooling. I scream bloody murder — the burn is so bad they rush me to the hospital.

Ants. Bank robbers. A burned bum.

But wait, here's the fourth picture.

Ah . . . *smile*. This is the best one. Me and my dad.

I lift it up close and peer in, remembering how good it felt — that warm-bright-bubbly time — so magical the Cinderella fairy dust of it sprinkles out over all the years before and after.

It is St. Patrick's Day and my parents are having a party. There are tinselly streamers hanging from the ceiling and decorations on the walls — shiny green shamrocks, leprechauns, rainbows with pots of gold. Irish music is playing loudly and the table is overflowing with meats, and salads, and desserts. My dad is pouring drinks and telling jokes with his best friend, Tommy Doyle. My pretty mom is giggling with her best friend, Ginny, both wearing swirly dresses and red lipstick. Everyone is eating and drinking, talking and laughing, singing and dancing. The whole room is happy, oh so happy. And I am in the center of it all, a princess perched on her throne.

In a green velvet dress, white tights, and black patent-leather shoes, I am sitting on top of the bar my daddy and Uncle Mark built. The wood is shellacked shiny smooth and there are four stools in front of it. I am propped between the beer steins named Schultz and Dooley. My daddy loves these funny guys. He flicks the little silver latches and makes their heads pop up and down like they're talking.

"Hello there, Aislinn, pass me the potato chips, will you?" Schultz says.

I giggle and feed Schultz a chip. "Here you go."

On my throne, swaying back and forth, kicking my heels, I munch one sticky sweet cherry after another from the dish by the bottles and bucket of ice.

A plastic drink-stirrer becomes my wand and I swoosh and point and tap it in the air, giving orders and granting wishes.

"Adorable," the guests say. "What a sweetheart you've got there, Roe!" My father is beaming proud. He winks and smiles; he loves me so much. I'm the heart of his world, his little girl.

"Come here, monkey." Dad scoops me in his arms.

He's "tipsy" but I know he won't drop me. He never does. We lead a "McNamara's Band" parade, I play the tuba, then drums, then cymbals with pot lids, then we do a jig again, until I'm giddy-dizzy and Daddy sets me back safe on my throne.

Right then someone *clicks* our picture, Daddy and me, happy together in this photo forever.

That's it. Four long-ago memories and zero sleep-dreams. But, luckily, I do have lots and lots of wide-awake dreams, and I'm saving three of the most important ones for this summer.

Two have a fair chance of coming true, one might take a miracle — but I have nine whole weeks to work on them before eighth grade starts in September.

1. I will find a way to stop Dad from drinking.
2. Mom will make him buy our house before it's too late.
3. Mike Mancinello will like me.

The first two dreams won't be easy, but the third dream . . . well, Mike Mancinello did say, "Sit here," *surprise*, on the bus home from school yesterday — it's amazing how you can know a boy since kindergarten and then *shazam-kabam*, it's like you just saw him for the very first time — and Mike did say, "Maybe I'll see you this summer, A."

And I did say, "That would be nice."

CHAPTER TWO
Summer School

I dream in my dream all the
dreams of the other dreamers . . .
— WALT WHITMAN

My full name is Aislinn Margaret-Elizabeth O'Neill, but everyone calls me A.

A. The first letter of the alphabet.

"A B C D E F G,

H I J K,

ella-mennow-pee,

Q R S,

T U V,

W, X, Y, and Z,

Now I know my ABC's

Next time won't you sing with me?"

My "class" and I just finished that rhyme. We sing it

every day with gusto when we begin the alphabet portion of summer school, right after the pledge of allegiance here in our classroom, which is really a shed.

I am the teacher. That's my biggest someday-dream.

"Nice job, B and C," I say, and my little brother Beck, and only sister, Callie, glow like sunbeams.

"You, too, D," I say, to my little brother Dooley, "you're getting it."

My brother Beck, we call him B, is five. He wants to be a professional baseball player, a starter for the Yankees. That's after he starts kindergarten in the fall.

Callie, we call her C, is four. She's a great dancer. She wants to be a ballerina some day. Callie got the dancing gene from our dad. He used to win jitterbug contests.

Dooley, D, is almost three, and fascinated with cars. He got that gene from our father, too. My dad is crazy about cars.

The youngest, Baby Eddie, E, he's one, is sitting up watching summer school from his portable playpen, teething on a plastic donut from his Fisher-Price sorting stack.

"B — blue," I say to Eddie, tapping on the blue donut.

"Boo," he says, giggling, chomping on it, drooling.

A, B, C, D, and E — it was my parents' idea to name us in alphabetical order. It seems every family's got a different way of naming kids. My cousins' names all start with M — Mitchell, Mary, Maura, and Matt. My other cousins all rhyme with "een" — Kathleen, Eileen, Maureen, and Noreen. My other cousins are all named after saints — Matthew, Mark, Luke, and John. (They should've been named after devils.)

The alphabetical order was my parents' idea but it was mine to nickname us letters. A, B, C, D, and E.

Our summer school shed is up behind our back porch. The whole property is on a hill. First the house, then the shed, then up farther the old boarded-up outhouse, then up higher the swing set, and then the pricker-bushes and the woods behind. The woods don't belong to Nana. I have my own secret place up there. It's called the Peely-Stick Shop.

My father built this shed. He's really good at building. The shed smells like lawnmower gasoline and grass clippings and car wax and it's cluttered with shovels and rakes, tires and tools, but I set up a nice enough classroom for us — me in the front with the green chalkboard easel I got for Christmas one year, and my students seated at the plastic chairs and table I bought cheap at the Hogans' garage sale.

Maizey Hogan is my best friend, ever since kindergarten.

The school shed isn't bright and cheerful like my real classroom will be someday. I wish I could hang up posters of the planets, a map of the world, pictures of presidents and other famous people, but there's no room. The walls are covered with tire hubcaps, rows and rows of hubcaps. My father collects them. That's his hobby.

"Okay, class. It's time for mathematics."

Eddie giggles and bites the red donut now. I give Beck and Callie the work sheets I made up special for them earlier, addition and subtraction problems, simple ones for Callie, harder for Beck since he's going to kindergarten. "Print your name carefully on the top line," I remind them. "Neatness counts."

I show Dooley how to hold his pencil. He's practicing making 4's this week.

Eddie's job is counting. Donuts.

"One . . . two . . . three," I say, stacking the blue, red, and yellow donuts.

"Boo," he says, picking up the blue donut.

"That's right," I say. "Good job, E, *blue*."

Callie whispers something to Beck and he points to something on her paper.

"Oh, right, B, thanks," she says, smiling at him with a look of total hero-worship.

I can't imagine what Callie is going to do when Beck goes to school in September. She keeps saying, "I'm going, too!" It's a shame she can't; she's ready.

B and C are like twins, they're so close. They do everything together, except ballet. Beck draws the line at tippy-toes and tutus. Callie's got no problem with baseball though. She's a super little slugger, blond wisps flying out beneath her cap.

"Finish up your work sheets, B and C," I say, "if you want time for recess. Daddy's coming home early today. We're driving Nana to the airport."

I look out the open door of our classroom at a squirrel scampering by. All summer long I'm going to have to babysit the little ones from the time when my mom leaves for work in the morning until she comes home at night. Not exactly how I want to spend my summer, but at least the teaching part will be fun. And Maizey will come over like she always does. We have a good time together, no matter what.

I'm going to call Maize when I get back from the

airport so we can make a plan for the weekend. Sometimes, when there's a firm plan, it's harder for my dad to say no.

No is his favorite word. It's simpler, one letter shorter than *y-e-s*, I guess.

Last summer Maizey came over every day. We'd spray the hose on the little ones to keep them cool, play jacks and onesie-twosie with a rubber ball against the house, listen to records and try to memorize the lyrics, and look at the Sears catalog, cutting out styles we liked.

This summer we're going to work on cheerleading routines so maybe we can make the team this fall. That, and plan how we'll celebrate our thirteenth birthdays. I'm October; Maizey is November. Teenagers, finally.

My nana usually helps babysit during the summer because she has time off from her job at Russell Sage College uptown. Nana irons the president's clothes and cleans the fancy student houses there. But this summer she's going to California, the whole opposite side of America from where we live in New York, to help out her daughter, my aunt Bitsy.

Aunt Bitsy is expecting her first baby and she's more jittery than a jitterbug. Her husband, Uncle Bobby, is a pilot in the air force in Vietnam and can't come home, so they sent money for a plane ticket so Nana can go help Aunt Bitsy "learn how to take care of a baby."

I don't think Nana wants to go at all. She rolls her eyes when anyone mentions it. "What's the big deal feeding a baby?" she says. "It's easy as milking a cow."

Nana was one of twelve children born on a dairy farm in Ireland. She learned to work hard young. Nana says Aunt Bitsy got so "book smart" in college that she turned "plain commonsense silly."

"All right," I say, ringing the little china bell I keep on my teacher desk. "Class dismissed until tomorrow. You may go play until Daddy gets home."

Beck and Callie run off up the hill past the outhouse to the two swings, one sliding board, and crooked teeter-totter set, Dooley trying admirably to keep up. "Wait for me!" D gets an A+ for effort, he does.

Eddie has just started toddling, but it's faster by far to carry him, so I scoop him up in my arms and then head into the house. I give him a bottle and put him in his crib.

When E falls asleep, I check that B, C, and D are doing okay, and then I walk down the back stairs to Nana's and rap on her kitchen window.

Nana comes to the door in a freshly pressed navy-blue

dress, wearing her pearl necklace and earrings, smelling like Emeraude perfume. Her suitcase is there on the floor, her fancy coat and hat on the hook. She's holding a prayer card.

"Come on in, angel," she says. "Just saying a novena." She looks at the clock. "Sit down. We've got time for tea."

There is always time for tea. Tea is my nana's answer to everything — a blizzard, a heat wave, the chicken pox, all ailments of the mind and body and heart.

CHAPTER THREE
On a Jet Plane

Swift as a shadow, short as any dream . . .
— SHAKESPEARE

Nana and I sit at her small, round kitchen table, looking out the window at the lilac bushes, which have now lost all their sweet-smelling purple buds.

Nana looks worried, scared even, her fingers fidgeting around her teacup. I know she's afraid of flying. She's never been on a plane before.

Nana rode a huge ocean liner across the Atlantic Ocean from Ireland all by herself when she was just sixteen, but ever since then her favorite vehicle is the city bus. Nana doesn't even like riding in my dad's car. She's always telling him to "slow down, Roe!"

And he does. My father listens when Nana talks. It's

almost like he's still a boy, not wanting to make his mommy mad. He loves her so much.

"Don't worry, Nana," I say. "I read once that people are safer riding a jet plane than they are riding in a car in their own neighborhood."

"Oh, no," Nana says, shaking her head vehemently, her lips pursed, like this is an absurd thing for me to say. "I'm not worried at all, dear." She refills my cup and then hers.

I know she's faking. That's the way Nana deals with things that trouble her. She makes believe they don't exist, or she says novenas.

Novenas are these really long prayers Catholics say. Nana's got a novena for everything — somebody's sick, somebody's dying, somebody lost their keys, somebody needs a wish granted.

I wonder what Nana wishes for? She never, ever says. We don't have those kinds of conversations. We talk about whether the tea is steeped enough, or does the soup needs salt, or if we think it will rain.

"When are you coming back?" I ask.

"Bitsy wants me to stay until Labor Day, but I told her I need to be home by the third week in August." Nana sets her cup down and winks at me.

Nana loves winking. She winks more than Santa Claus.

"We have a date, don't we?" Nana says, walking to the wall calendar and flipping up the pages. "August twenty-first — Aislinn. Got it circled right here."

"Yes!" I say, smiling, relieved that she didn't forget. Nana and I have an annual date — the third Saturday of August. It's a tradition.

Ever since I started kindergarten, Nana and I take the bus uptown and we go to Cooper's Shoe Store and Nana buys me whichever pair I choose — no matter the cost — and that's very generous of her because I know she isn't rich. Nana says shoes are a person's most important apparel purchase. "You can sew a patch on a pocket or let the hem out on a skirt, but a girl should start a new school year in shoes she's proud of."

After we get the shoes (we never buy anything besides the shoes) we go to a restaurant for lunch — Fatone's or Manory's or the Puritan — and we get a booth and take our time looking over the menu and placing our orders (we're never in a rush; it's such a good feeling), and we generally order tuna fish sandwiches with potato chips and extra pickles and we always, always order pie for dessert, with tea, of course.

Sometimes when we're having our annual back-to-school lunch, my new shoes in a box on the seat beside me, and lots of times when I'm sitting here across the table from Nana, here in her kitchen, sometimes I think, *Go ahead, A, do it. . . . Ask Nana for help. Tell Nana how bad it's getting. How scared you are.*

But then I don't. Because I know that Nana already knows how bad it is.

Often, when we're sitting here having tea, we can hear the little ones' feet pounding, running back and forth upstairs, Dad yelling, sometimes the sharp yelp and crying after someone's been spanked, Dad shouting at Mom, doors slamming.

Nana hears Dad ridiculing my mom about her cooking or her weight in front of everyone at Sunday dinner. She's seen him hit us, watched him stumble up the stairs after a night out at a bar; she's listened to me complain about him not letting me go anywhere, locked up like a prisoner, always having to babysit, not being able to join my friends for movies or the seventh-grade end-of-year dance last week. ("It's not a date, Dad, it's just a dance!") I didn't even know then that Mike Mancinello might like me; I just wanted to have fun with my class, just like everybody else.

Nana's watched me sit here crying, tears dripping down on this table, heart broken over and over again, and yet she never says a bad word about him. It's like there are red lights swirling and alarms blaring and megaphones booming "evacuate! evacuate!" on the floor right above her in this house that she owns with this family she loves so much and she can smell the smoke, but she pours another cup of tea, says another novena, and refuses to shout "fire!"

Suddenly I am very scared about Nana leaving for the whole summer. I will be the only one home during the day with all of the little ones. And even though Nana never yells at my father, I know that if something really, *really* bad happened upstairs I could run right down here and get her. . . .

Maybe now . . . I try to meet her eyes. . . . *Maybe now since she's leaving for the whole summer, maybe she would say something to him before she goes.* My heart beats faster. *Do it, A, now.*

"Nana?" I say.

"Yes, darling?"

Beep, beep, beep. The loud honking of a car horn shatters the quiet and makes both of us jump in our seats. My father's home, impatiently honking in the driveway;

he doesn't like to be kept waiting. *Beep, beep, beep.* I stand, my heart pounding. Any time he comes home, my heart pounds. One has to be on guard.

"Oh, dear," Nana says, looking at the clock.

I shout for B, C, and D to hurry down from the swings, and I rush up the steps. "Time to go to the airport!" I wake up Eddie, quickly change his diaper, grab the sack I packed earlier with snacks and toys for the road, and lead them all down to the car.

Nana squeezes in the backseat with us, her knuckles snow-white, clutching her purse in her lap. I can feel her fear.

Callie sits on Beck's lap. Dooley climbs on Nana's. I've got baby E.

Dooley offers Nana an animal cracker from his box. "It's a lion, Nana," he says.

"Oh, no, dear, thank you," she says.

D's hand plunges in the box and out again. "Here, Nana. How 'bout a camel?"

Nana is lost in thought. I smile at Dooley. "I'll take it, D. I love camels."

At the airport, we say good-bye on the sidewalk. Nana slips me a taped-up note. "Open it later," she whispers with a wink. I stick it in my pocket.

"And please remember to water and weed my flowers."

"Okay, Nana. Don't worry. Good luck! Tell Aunt Bitsy we said hi. Send me a picture of the baby and San Francisco, too!"

We hug quickly; Nana's not big on hugging. I start to cry. It's the first time Nana's ever gone away from us. The first time someone in my family has taken off on an airplane. The first time I've ever been to an airport. *Where are all these people going?*

Dad drives us to a parking area and turns off the ignition. We watch a few planes take off. Maybe one of them is Nana's. *Be strong, Nana. You'll be fine. "I'm leaving on a jet plane, don't know when I'll be back again."* That Peter, Paul and Mary song I like flits through my mind. Oh, how I'd love to leave on a jet plane, fly off to California. To anywhere. With Maizey, of course, or maybe Mike Man . . .

My father turns around and looks at me.

It's as if he heard my mind talking.

"Ready, Freddies?" he says, meaning ready to go home.

B, C, and D giggle. They all know Dad's talking about Freddy Freihofer, that guy on TV who draws pictures for kids and then gives them Freihofer's chocolate chip cookies.

Driving home, Dad screeches on the brakes, flips on the blinking lights, and swerves our red convertible off to the side of the road so fast E nearly topples off my lap.

This can only mean one thing.

CHAPTER FOUR
Hubcaps, the GANE, and Cinderella

Such sights as youthful poets dream on summer eves . . .
— MILTON

S it tight, I'll be right back," Dad tells us, all squeezed like sausage links in a frying pan in this hot, cramped backseat. It would be cooler if the top was down, but Mom made Dad promise he wouldn't do that with all of us in the backseat. He drives so fast she's afraid somebody will fall out.

Beck and Callie giggle-tease each other and play the itsy-bitsy spider finger rhyme I taught them. Dooley eats a monkey cracker, then races his favorite red Matchbox car, *vroom, vroom, vroom,* up and down Eddie's leg. Eddie giggles and tries to swipe the car.

Me? I follow my father like a hawk. *What does he see in those hubcaps?*

Sticking my head out the window, I watch him pick up the silver circle, look in it as if it's a mirror, his face aglow like a kid on his birthday. He turns it around in his hands, studying it. My dad knows every make and model of every car there is.

Our car was probably real sharp when he first got it, and Dad takes good care polishing it every Saturday for what seems like hours, but no amount of wax can polish away the rust.

Dad wants to buy a new car; that's his really big dream. I hear Mom and Dad arguing about it. Dad wants a Cadillac, the most expensive car of all, but Mom says we need a station wagon and besides, we need to save every penny for our house.

I open the note from Nana. There are two quarters taped on the paper. "For a treat," she wrote. Nana's always giving me two quarters taped up tight like it's gold.

When we get home, Dad heads straight to the shed to hang up his new hubcap. He's got a whole hubcap gallery, carefully arranged and polished and hung in neat rows. He's prouder of those hubcaps than of me, I think.

Mom is home from work, in the kitchen frying

hamburgers for dinner. Her face is puffy and there are circles under her eyes. Dooley runs to clutch her legs.

"You look exhausted, Mom," I say.

"I'm fine, honey." She smiles at me. "Nana get off okay?"

"Yep." I race to call Maizey before Dad comes down from the shed. He doesn't like us talking on the phone. "A customer might be trying to call me," he says.

Mrs. Hogan answers. "Oh, sorry, A, Maizey's still at the pool with Sue-Ellen."

Sue-Ellen? My enemy? That snotty, awful girl who made fun of me in front of the whole class in fourth grade? *What is Maizey doing with her?*

After dinner, Dad gargles with Listerine, slaps on some Old Spice Cologne, and puts on a new shirt and tie and his blue suit jacket. Then he takes one of the HELLO MY NAME IS labels from his desk and writes *ROE*.

"I've got a meeting," Dad says and leaves.

It's probably a sales meeting or that Toastmasters club he belongs to where people learn how to talk confidently in public and win prizes for giving speeches. I just hope he comes right home after instead of going to a bar.

Mom washes the dishes and I dry, then I sweep the kitchen floor. Mom gives E his bath. Maizey still hasn't called. I try her number again. This time Mr. Hogan answers. "No, dear," he says, "she's having dinner at some girl's house."

Oh, no. That's it. I've got to get to the bottom of this. When did Maizey start being so friendly with Sue-Ellen? And why didn't Maizey call me? *Is she mad at me? Did I do something wrong?*

Halfheartedly, I play Barrel of Monkeys with B and C until Mom comes to take them for their baths. I read Dooley his favorite book, about a steam shovel, twice, then I tuck him in and kiss his cheek, smiling at the red Matchbox car clutched in his little fist.

Later I find Mom asleep at the kitchen table, her head resting on her arms folded atop her typewriter. Every night Mom tries to write another page of her book. My mom was going to go to college and be a famous writer but she got married instead. All day long she works in a "typing pool" — not a swimming pool, no, that would be fun — this is a bunch of ladies sitting in rows wearing headphones listening to words that lawyers have taped — and she types out nice, clean, perfectly spelled sentences.

Mom has to type exactly what she hears, no trying to make things sound better. She is "paid to type, not to write." Mom said her boss made that very clear. That's too bad, really, a crying shame, because my mother is the most spectacular writer ever. Her poems are like paintings and she writes the most beautiful messages on my birthday cards and holiday cards that make me feel so good.

My mother's dream is to write a "great book." I tell her I think it will be the Greatest American Novel Ever, the GANE, I call it. She laughs and shakes her head.

Too bad I missed seeing my mother writing tonight. Sometimes when I hear those little typewriter keys clickety-clacking I'll go to the kitchen for some water just so I can see the look on her face. That's when my mom seems youngest, prettiest, happiest of all — when she's writing — peaceful like the faces of the saint statues up at church.

My mother is snoring. I tap her arm gently.

"Oh, A, honey, thanks," she says, yawning. "I've got to go to bed. You, too."

She puts her typewriter in its case and stuffs her stack of papers in the box, then puts them both back in the pantry above the canned goods shelf.

My father still isn't home. I try Maizey's number again.

"Oh, hi, A," she says. Her voice sounds strange.

"Where were you all day?" I say.

"Doing stuff with Sue-Ellen."

"But . . ." I stop, waiting for her to say she's sorry.

"Listen, A, don't be mad," Maizey says. "You're still my best friend, it's just . . . I don't want to spend my whole summer doing nothing again."

Nothing?

When my head hits the pillow, I lay awake listening for my father. Finally, I hear the tires crunching on the gravel driveway down below, his footsteps across the back porch, the kitchen door unlocking, keys jangling down on the table, the cupboard opening, bottle clanking on the counter, the refrigerator opening, ice tinkling in a glass, liquor being poured. The sounds are like music, a tune I know by heart.

I sit up in bed to listen better. I have become quite excellent at listening. My ears are like battleship receptors set to detect the slightest enemy sound.

Mom comes out to the kitchen and they're talking. "Good night, then," she says. I hear the television turning on, Dad laughing about something. He goes to the kitchen for another drink. And then it's just the TV for a long time. Soon he'll fall asleep on the couch. "Good night, Flop," I whisper to my stuffed rabbit with the missing ear.

Some hours later, my bedroom door swings open with a *bang* against the wall. There is no lock on my and Callie's door. We have to stuff a sock between the door and frame and pull the knob shut to keep it closed. I sit up startled, heart booming.

My dad's in the doorway, yelling at me. His HELLO MY NAME IS *ROE* sticker has slipped off onto his sleeve and is curling around the edges.

"Get out of that bed. Get out in that kitchen and sweep that floor right now. It's filthy. There's crumbs all over." He's wobbling back and forth.

"Sure, Dad, okay," I say softly so as not to wake up Callie. She gets so scared when he acts like this. I move past my father, smelling his Old Spice Cologne and booze and I walk to the kitchen for the broom.

There are no crumbs. I do not argue. I can handle this, easy as pie. All I need to do is sweep the floor, sweep the floor, simple as Cinderella.

He's drunk and mad and I won't make him madder, simple as Cinderella.

CHAPTER FIVE
Morning Jailbreak

Whatever you can do or dream you can, begin it:
Boldness has genius, power and magic in it.
— JOHANN WOLFGANG VON GOETHE

In the morning I wake up to the sound of my father throwing up in the bathroom, the room right next to mine and Callie's.

Good, serves you right for drinking so much, waking me up to sweep imaginary crumbs off the floor. Otherwise our house is quiet.

It's not "our house," of course, it's Nana's — white with green trim, two floors and a basement, steep stairs down to the city sidewalk and four lanes of traffic, two zipping toward and two zipping off the bridge, which runs over the Hudson River.

Our very short street begins at the bridge and ends on the corner where we live. There are four houses, but there might as well be none, since we never see our neighbors. The couple next door are always working, and they don't have children; then there's the family with the cluttered yard full of toys and appliances; then the house where I once played the Game of Life with a teenage granddaughter who was visiting from Ohio. Beyond that is a stone fence, about as tall as Beck, with a narrow opening I know I could squeeze through if I got the chance, leading down a grassy bank to the oil tankers and the railroad tracks that run beneath the bridge, alongside the river.

I'm not allowed near the river. Nana says "hoboes and tramps" live there. I think she's exaggerating.

We're crowded up here on the top floor of Nana's house, but it's the White House compared to the basement where Mom and Dad and I started out. At least now we have windows, eight of them. In the winter, when the leaves have fallen, from the window in the small yellow bedroom that Callie and I share, if I stand on my tippy-toes and crank my neck *just so*, I can see a sliver of the river.

It looks so pretty, that river — so free and flowing — like I could sail away or skip away or skate away on it somewhere *happily ever after.*

I would love to stick my fingers in that river, look in to see if there are fish, scoop some water up in my hand, just to see what it feels like.

My alarm clock says seven A.M. The toilet flushes. The water runs. There's the *tap, tap, tap* of his razor against the porcelain sink. My pet turtle, Frisky, is standing up in his pool house trying to peek over the side.

My father is an auto-parts salesman, a really good one. He's always getting trophies. He and Mom even won a trip to the Bahamas once. Dad likes to make sales calls when his customers are just opening their gas stations and repair shops for the day. He brings them donuts or warm Danish pastries from Nelligan's bakery. I used to go with him sometimes, not anymore though.

Hopefully Dad will make good commissions this month, enough to finally put the down payment on our house. He keeps telling Mom "we're close, we're close," and she keeps saying "please, Roe, soon; somebody else is going to make an offer."

"Our house" is out in the country, about a twenty-minute ride from here. It's a big brick house with a porch and two chimneys and a grassy field big enough to play a real baseball game in and so many trees for hide-and-seek that no one would ever find me. There's a stream where we'll swim and float on rafts and there are apple trees, six of them, I counted, apple pie all year long.

The place needs "a ton of work," Dad says, but he's not afraid of "a little elbow grease." We stop by to check on it nearly every Sunday when Dad takes us out for a drive. B, C, and D race to the tire swing hanging from that thick tree limb or they toss pebbles into the stream. Mom plans where she'll plant a vegetable garden. Dad scopes out the perfect spot for a garage to hold the classic cars he wants to own one day and another spot where he promises to build my mother her very own little "writer's house."

Me? I rub dirt from the windows and look inside.

There's a huge stone fireplace, furniture covered with sheets, bookshelves from floor to ceiling, a crystal chandelier, and a wide staircase leading upstairs. I'm guessing from all the windows I've counted — there are sixteen — that there might even be enough bedrooms up there, or maybe up in the attic, for me to have a room of my own.

"Are you sure we can afford it, Roe?" Mom says to Dad.

"Of course, Mags," he answers, not a care in the world, like he's Daddy Warbucks. "I've got a special account all set up. Don't worry. I'm going to take good care of my girl. That's a promise." Mom blushes when he calls her "my girl."

There's been a FOR SALE sign on our house for two years now. Every time we pull up the driveway, I hold my breath, afraid the words will have changed to SOLD.

Dad says he's almost got enough money, "just a few more good commissions."

My mother keeps getting more and more anxious that someone will buy the house before we do (I considered taking the FOR SALE sign home with us last time, but my conscience got the better of me). Dad says, "Stop worrying, will you, Mags? This place isn't going anywhere. It's way overpriced. It needs a new roof, new windows . . ."

I think maybe Dad's waiting for just the right time to surprise us. He loves surprising us, like last Christmas when I really, really wanted a guitar and nearly cried when there wasn't one under the tree on Christmas morning.

"Maybe Santa forgot, A," Beck tried consoling me.

"Maybe next year if you're better," Callie said.

Everybody opened their presents and we finished breakfast and we were just about to leave for church when Dad went into his closet-office (I call it that because it's supposed to be a coat closet) and he came out with a big box. "What's this?" he said, looking all confused. "It's got your name on it, A." He smiled at Mom.

"My guitar! Oh, thank you, Dad!" I hugged him. He had tears in his eyes.

Dad likes playing Santa Claus. He likes being the hero.

Maybe this Sunday we'll drive to our house and Dad will hand Mom the keys and say, "It's all yours now, babe." Or maybe it will be on Mom's birthday next month . . . or their anniversary. That way we could still be moved in and settled by the time school starts and then have our first Thanksgiving there, turkey with trimmings and apple pie, of course.

I hear the kitchen door close, then the car starting up in the driveway down below.

"A?" My mom is calling me. She gently pushes open my bedroom door. "Will you go to the store for me?"

"Sure," I say. It's a way to escape this house for a while. My dad keeps me locked up here like I'm in prison. I can't ride my bike past the park. I can't leave the yard without permission. I can't go out at night. I can't talk to boys or go on dates. "When you're in high school," he says.

I put on a top and some shorts and sneakers. Maybe I have time to stop by Maizey's house, too. She's usually up early like me.

In the kitchen, my mother is pouring milk into Dooley's cereal bowl. D is racing his red car around the bowl and then the sugar bowl and his juice glass, too. *Vroom, eeeek, vroom, vroom.* "Careful, Dool," Mom says.

Eddie's in his highchair, kicking his chubby legs against the table. Mom shakes a few Cheerios onto his tray and he sets to picking up the O's between his thumb and pointer fingers with an expression of great determination.

"I need you to get a quart of milk and . . ." Mom stops talking and runs to the sink. She coughs and spits, then throws up.

"Mom! . . . are you okay?" I move toward her, reach out to touch her back.

My mother spits again. She turns on the faucet and splashes water on her face. As she dries herself with a dish towel she glances out at the bird feeder she suction-cupped back on the window now that Nana's gone to California. Nana had told Mom to remove it because she said the seeds were floating down past Nana's kitchen window to the ground and luring up rats from the river.

Mom said the rat part was ridiculous. She said it under her breath, but I heard her.

Good for Mom sticking that bird feeder back out there now that Nana's gone to California. It's nice to see the birds again.

A tiny brown bird lands, *peck-peck*s a few seeds, then *whee* is off again, free.

"I'm fine, A," Mom says, sighing a long, loud sigh. She turns and looks at me.

As soon as I see her eyes, I know.

She's pregnant. Number six is on the way. "You're having another baby? Oh, Mom, no! You can't! You almost died with Dooley and Eddie. . . ."

"Shhh," Mom says, looking at D, but he's too busy speeding to pay attention.

"Careful, Dooley, you're making a mess," I say, grabbing a rag to sop up the goop before it sticks to the linoleum and I'll have to work extra hard scrubbing it off later. "Mom, *why*? The doctor told you not to have any more. . . ."

When my mother is expecting, her blood pressure soars and her body swells up and near the end all she can do is lie on the couch like a beached whale, uncomfortable and worried, waiting.

"It'll be a November baby," she says quietly.

"Oh," I mumble. What else can I say? My mother doesn't look like I should say congratulations. This doesn't feel like a happy moment.

Mom wipes her mouth and studies her face in the little round mirror hanging from a nail above the sink. Strange place for a mirror, but sometimes Dad takes such a long time in the bathroom with his "nervous stomach" that one of us will need to brush our teeth in the kitchen.

My mother moves a strand of brown hair off of her forehead and *slap-pat-pats* her cheeks to bring some color. My mother used to be so beautiful, but now she's pale as laundry-line sheets, and tired and pudgy, older. She doesn't dress up nice anymore, black stretch pants and smock tops mostly. I can't remember the last time she wore lipstick.

"First!" Dooley shouts, swooping an imaginary race flag. The cereal bowl topples to the floor. "Ooh, sorry," he says, so genuinely remorseful it's hard to get mad at him.

"Hand me my pocketbook, A," Mom says, motioning to the counter.

Mom fishes out her wallet, calculates the cost, and counts out the money. "Get a loaf of bread and a pound of cheese. You can do grilled cheese for lunch again."

Good. I am a spectacular grilled-cheese maker. My secret is that I add a little "something extra" each time. When the butter's melted in the frying pan and I put down the bottom bread slices and then lay on the cheese, I'll sprinkle on some shredded bits of ham or bologna or sliced tomatoes or pickles before I put on the rooftop slices of bread. Once, I added peaches with a little spicy mustard. It was delicious.

Beck and Callie think it's so exciting when I make grilled cheese. They sit at the kitchen table watching me like television.

"Whad'she put in there this time?" one of them will ask the other.

"I don't know. Whatdaya think?"

"I don't know. Guess."

Yesterday, the refrigerator was empty, but I found a slice of sausage pizza left in the freezer from Callie's birthday. *Hmm. . . .* I let the slice thaw out and then I chopped it up good and spooned the crumbles evenly on each of our sandwiches.

"This is your best one yet, A," Beck said with conviction.

I felt proud.

"Here," my mother says, giving me a quarter. "Buy yourself a donut."

"Thanks, Mom." Jelly donuts are my very favorite. Whoever invented them was a genius.

"You and those donuts," Mom smiles, touching my cheek.

I get the quarters Nana gave me so I can buy Maizey a donut, too. I need to tell her I'm sorry for acting so cold on the phone last night and invite her to come over today. When the little ones are napping we can start working on our tans or practice our cheerleading moves.

"Hurry back, A," Mom says, looking at the clock. "I need to get ready for work."

And off I go on my morning jailbreak.

All points bulletin, alert, alert, Inmate Number 1, Aislinn aka "Dream" O'Neill, is escaping the prison yard. The convict is armed with quarters and is known to be fond of donuts. . . . Jelly.

CHAPTER SIX
Seagulls

Whales in mid-ocean,
suspended in the waves of the sea . . .
And dreaming with strange whale eyes wide open . . .
— D. H. LAWRENCE

Outside, I hurry down the back steps, past Nana's flowers, nodding to the little gnome statues — "Red," with the red cap and white beard reading a book, and "Green," with the green cap and brown beard hoisting a beer stein. "You should stop drinking," I scold and pull my bike out from behind the garbage cans.

Wheeling my bike down the side of the house, across the lawn and our gravelly driveway to the city sidewalk, I take deep breaths of morning air, feeling *free, free, free,* bubbling up inside. When it reaches my throat I open my mouth and a song flies out:

Up, up with people!

You meet them wherever you go

Up, up with people!

They're the best kind of folks we know. . . .

Miss McMahon taught us that song in fifth grade. I loved Miss McMahon with her beehive hairdo and crazy-patterned minidresses, blue eye shadow and shiny pink lipstick. Every morning she would smile and raise her hands like a conductor and our whole class would stand up and sing that song, belt it out loud, swaying our hips and clapping our hands like we were on *The Ed Sullivan Show* on TV. Boy, were we good.

Every once in a while, our principal, Sister Benedict James, in her black-and-white penguin dress with the brown rosary beads and crucifix belt, would *rap-rap-rap* on the window, then open the door and stick in her pruney face all scrunched in a scowl and Miss McMahon would nod respectfully and say, "Good morning, Sister James," then turn to us and say, "Okay, people, down we go."

Up, up with people!

You meet them wherever you go

Up, up with people!

They're the best kind of folks we know

If more people were FOR people

All people everywhere

There'd be a lot less people to worry about

And a lot more people who'd care.

Miss McMahon was the teacher who made me want to be a teacher someday. She also inspired my singing. One time she said, "Aislinn, you have a beautiful voice." I'll always remember that moment. That's what a teacher can do for someone. Miss McMahon moved away before I could tell her how much I loved her. Miss McMahon was so kind, I almost told her about Dad's drinking.

It was right around fifth grade, when our class moved up to the upper-grades floor at school, that things really started getting bad at home. My dad was drinking every night now, not just the weekends anymore. He had switched from beer to liquor and, after three or four drinks, if something made him mad, he'd start shouting and swearing, his face so red it looked like he'd explode. I tried harder than ever to keep him happy, to keep the mad from crossing over to the madder. I would come home from school, quick do my homework, help make dinner, clean up the kitchen, read stories, give baths, tuck the little ones into bed, then lie awake, wide, wide awake, listening until I knew he'd conked out on the couch and we were safe. . . .

Turning my bike at the corner, I nearly collide with Mike Mancinello.

Mike Mancinello!

"Hi, A," he says, smiling, his long brown bangs dipping down over his hot-cocoa brown eyes. He's wearing jeans and a Yankees T-shirt, a gold chain around his neck. There's an empty canvas sack in the basket; he must have been delivering papers.

Oh my gosh. My heart goes *pitter-patter-flippity-flip-flop*. Mike Mancinello, the nicest, smartest, funniest, cutest boy in the world is smiling at me. Me. Me. Me.

Mike looks nervous, like he doesn't know what to say. Gosh knows, I don't either. I think of how he said "sit here if you want" on the bus the other day when that awful Sue-Ellen had taken my seat next to Maizey. *My seat, with my best friend, Maizey.*

I should have seen it coming. Sue-Ellen started out bribing Maizey with packs of gum and then she invited her to watch a show on her brand-new color console. Maizey asked if I could come, too, but I had to go straight home, *of course*. I try being nice to Sue-Ellen, truly I do, but after what she did to me in fourth grade . . . when I saw Sue-melon-face sitting in my seat, *my seat* next to Maizey, I was so blood-boiling jealous I thought I might scratch her face or worse, start crying, and then Mike said "sit here if you want, A," and suddenly bluebirds were singing.

"Okay, well . . . see ya," Mike says, shrugging his shoulders, looking confused.

His voice jolts me back to the moment but off he pedals, before I can pop a *hello* or *good-bye* or any decent word out of my mouth.

Jeesh. What is the matter with me? I was so busy thinking, I forgot to talk. I hope he didn't think I was rude. What if he thinks I don't like him? Him, the boy who helped me with math. Him, the boy who really listened when I read my rainbow poem in front of the class and clapped, *clapped*, when I was finished. Who knows when I'll get another chance to talk to him? I can never go places where boys might be. My father won't let me talk to boys, not even on the telephone.

The sidewalk pavement is bumpy and cracked with little shaggy grass islands springing up here and there, where only smooth pavement should be. I focus on not swerving into the road, where cars are whooshing past me on their way to important places. My father doesn't let me ride my bike around the city, but Mom does when he's away. "What he doesn't know won't hurt him," she says.

I head past the park where we have our Town Picnic in August. There's a flurry of white in the sky and then a flock of seagulls swoops down. *Seagulls.* They look so funny here, little misfits, far away from their ocean home.

On cool mornings like this after a hot night, sometimes there's a foggy mist over the park and if I look close I see tiny dewdrops glistening on the grass. I stop and watch a gull dip its head *sip, sip, sip*ping drops so different from the humongous sea it's used to.

Seagull, such a pretty word. Before I knew that having more babies could kill my mother, I once told Mom and Dad that when they got to G in the alphabet, they should "name the G one Gull." Dad burst out laughing, holding his stomach, tears in his eyes. Mom rolled her eyes and sighed. *I wonder if Mom told him about the new baby yet?*

Someday I would love to see the sea. It looks spectacular on TV, and oh what a beautiful sound it makes!

My uncle Tommy, aunt Flo, and the saints, they're rich, have a lake camp up north and I love swimming there, especially in the morning before the motorboats roar. The lake water is cool and peaceful and silky-soft on my skin. But the sea? The sea looks like it would shake you right up, all those waves and bubbles and foam. I bet seawater is sizzly, maybe it tickles and makes you laugh. I would love to know how it feels to swim in the ocean so I could compare it to a lake. Mom and Dad keep promising a beach vacation "someday," but with saving all the money for our house, and a car, and now with another baby coming, I don't think that's ever going to happen.

An engine *rrr-rrr-rev*s up and a man rides a lawn mower out of the park maintenance building. The seagulls lift up and fly off noisily, *caw, caw, caw*. I wave as they pass over my head. A feather floats down. I pick it up. Maybe it's a sign.

Mrs. Garbowski's store smells like donuts, yum. Maria Carroll is just leaving. "Aislinn, hello!" she says, so happy to see me.

Maria Carroll is the prettiest, nicest lady ever. She and her husband, Leo, live across the street from our church. They are the youngest married people I know.

The Carrolls always buy four instead of one of the giant candy bars I have to sell every year to raise money for our school. Back when I sold Girl Scout cookies they bought two of every flavor. And when I sell Christmas cards through that catalog in the fall, Maria orders the most expensive line, three boxes, and I make a nice bonus.

I don't think the Carrolls are rich or anything, they are just really kind to me. Whenever I call on them selling something, Maria always insists I "have a bite to eat and visit for a while." She makes amazing lasagna, and sugar cookies the size of my hand.

Maria has a satchel on her shoulder with a peace symbol on it. "I start school today, A," she says, excited.

"College?" I say.

"Yep, I'm taking a psychology course at Hudson Valley. Getting my feet wet before I go full-time in the fall. Say a prayer for me." She laughs. "It's been a few years since I was a student."

"Oh, you'll do fine," I say.

"Stop up and visit us soon, okay?" Maria says. "We miss you."

"Sure," I say. "Good luck!"

Mrs. Garbowski puts my groceries in a bag and the donuts in a separate little white bag, tucking in a napkin. "In case you want one on the road," she says, smiling.

I put the bags in my basket and set off. Waiting for the light on the corner by Maizey's street, I lift out a donut and take a bite. *Hmmm.* The sugary powder coats my lips and the sweet grape jelly glides over my tongue, *yum.* Someday when I have money I'm going to buy myself a whole dozen of these every week, no, every day. I wonder how jelly would taste in grilled cheese?

"Hey, A . . . A!" Someone's calling me. *Maizey.*

"Hi!" I wave, so happy to see her. "I was just coming to your house."

Maizey's leaning out the window of a brand-new Cadillac. I know because the catalog is on our living room table. Dooley spilled grape juice all over it and boy did he get spanked. This isn't Maizey's family's car. The Hogans have a blue station wagon.

"Where are you going?" I shout.

Before Maizey can answer, Snoop-Melon's face is in the window, too.

"The country club," Snoop shouts all happy, pushing her sunglasses up to make a hair band like the movie stars do.

I didn't ask you.

"We're going to have breakfast and take a tennis lesson and then Maize and I are going to swim and sunbathe on the lounge chairs while my mom plays golf. Then we're going to have lunch out on the member's-only terrace dining room and . . ."

I wipe jelly from my chin, *stupid donut.* The light turns green and the Cadillac moves forward. *Why didn't Maizey call me to say they were going?* Not that I could have gone anyway.

Maizey looks sad, but not too sad, as she waves good-bye to me.

I stuff the rest of the donut back in the bag, scrunch it into a ball, toss it in my basket. Here I am headed back to the jailhouse and my best friend is off for a day of fun with the snottiest girl in the world. This is so unfair. My father has no right to keep me locked up like a criminal. I'm going to find a way to get out. He is the meanest father ever . . . but that's not the only feeling making that donut swirl sick in my stomach.

Am I losing Maizey? She and Snoop-Melon will have the whole long summer together, to go swimming, shopping, to the movies. I know Maizey loves me, but why would she still be my friend when she can have so much more fun at a country club?

CHAPTER SEVEN
Confession

But I, being poor, have only my dreams;
I have spread my dreams under your feet;
Tread softly because you tread on my dreams.
— WILLIAM BUTLER YEATS

On Saturday morning, Dad is all cheerful in the kitchen. He touches Mom's stomach. "Did you hear the good news, A?" he says to me.

Dad is always so happy when they are expecting a baby. He loves babies. It's when they get older and start running around making noise and saying what they want and getting into mischief that he loses patience with them.

I take advantage of his good mood. "Can I go to Maizey's?" I ask.

"Sure," he says. "Sure, why not?"

I bike quickly to Maizey's and ring the doorbell.

"Sorry, A," Mrs. Hogan says. "She's off with Sue-Ellen already."

When I get home, my father's polishing his car, the radio blaring, him whistling along. I go write in my diary, a new wish that Dad will let me go somewhere fun with Maizey tomorrow, maybe Hoffman's Playland. I put the diary key in a new spot, the pocket of my elf, Jeffrey's, green felt jacket. I keep changing the key location, just to be safe.

At four o'clock my father yells to me, "A, you ready?"

"Yep."

Every Saturday afternoon at four o'clock, I have to go to confession with my father. Confession is one of the seven sacraments of the Catholic Church. You tell your sins to a priest and then your soul gets clean so you can receive Communion on Sunday.

Even though our church, Saint Michael the Archangel, is just up the hill from our house, an easy walk, Dad says "let's take the car." After all that polishing, I guess he wants to show it off.

He puts the top down. I sit up front where my mom usually sits. Mom doesn't come to confession. She has to watch the little ones. Besides, I don't think she sins.

Two winters ago we had a blizzard and school was canceled and the roads were closed. Dad got out an Easter photograph of me, Mom, and Callie with our new dresses and the corsages he bought us standing on the church steps waving and said, "Want me to teach you how to draw?"

"Yes!"

Dad and I sat there at the kitchen table for hours, him teaching me things like "perspective" and "scale" as we drew. My mom made us sandwiches and hot cocoa.

We never finished that picture. Someday, maybe.

The church is brown with tall spires and stained-glass windows. We walk up the steps and my father yanks open the heavy door. A spicy aroma, incense and candles, whooshes out over us like a veil. It's dark and quiet. There's the old man in the brown suit with the gray feather in his hat in his same spot in the last row. He's always there, like he lives here or something. I don't know his name. He's always hunched over praying when we get to church and he's already gone when we leave. I recognize a few people, no one my age.

We dip our fingers into the holy-water fountain, make

the sign of the cross on our foreheads, and then kneel in a pew.

Bowing my head and closing my eyes, I try to remember exactly what sins I told the priest, Father Reilly, last week so I don't say the same sins again because then he might think I was lying last week, which actually I was because I just make up sins to tell him because what else would I have to say to the guy when I go in that dark wooden closet small as the take-your-picture booth at Woolworth's?

Nana's friend Mrs. Casey, the bank robber, *smile*, comes out of the confessional and Dad nudges my arm to go ahead in. As she passes by me and smiles, I notice Mrs. Casey has a Kleenex tissue bobby-pinned on her head to make like a hat. Nana does that, sometimes, too. Women and girls are supposed to wear hats in church. Men and boys must remove their hats, even baseball caps. Frankly, all the hat rules seem silly to me. I wonder if God really cares. Seems to me God's got more important things to worry about, like the war in Vietnam, for instance, than keeping track of who's wearing a hat or not. I think of my uncle Bobby and my mom's brother, Uncle Jimmy, both serving in the war. *Please, God, bring them home safely.*

I enter the dark closet of the confessional and draw the brown curtain closed behind me. I kneel down on the cushion, and fold my hands.

On the other side of the murky screen, Father Reilly keeps his head faced forward so he can pretend he doesn't know it's me, which of course is silly because he knows it's me because I'm here the same time every Saturday, and he always says "I'll see you at Mass tomorrow, Aislinn," after he doles out my penance.

I make the sign of the cross and start in . . . "Oh, my God, I am heartily sorry for having offended thee. It's been one week since my last confession. These are my sins."

I say that I lied two times and disobeyed my parents three times and was "uncharitable" to my sister and brothers four times. There, that was sufficiently different from last Saturday. That ought to keep him happy.

"Is that everything?" Father Reilly says in a quiet voice.

"Yes, Father." What else can I say? All you can talk about in here is what you did wrong. It's not the place to talk about what your father's doing wrong, for instance.

Father Reilly mumbles a short prayer. *I wonder what*

he's saying? Then he gives me my penance. "Say three Hail Marys, two Our Fathers, and a Glory Be."

"Yes, Father. Thank you, Father."

"I'll see you at Mass tomorrow, Aislinn."

When Dad sees me coming back to the pew, he stands up to take his turn.

I kneel back down in our pew, make the sign of the cross, and say my penance, "Hail Mary: Full of grace, the Lord is with thee. . . ." Then "Our Father who art in heaven . . ." Then "Glory be to the Father, and to the Son, and to the Holy Spirit . . ." and then I tell God I'm sorry for the only real sin I made, which was just now lying to the priest about sinning, and then I sit back on the seat to wait.

It's musty and shadowy in here; the big overhead chandeliers are off to keep it cooler during the summer. The only light is what's coming in through the stained glass windows and the flickering flames of the votive candles people pay money to light when they want God to help a sick person get better or speed a loved one out of purgatory.

Purgatory is where dead people go who had sins left on their souls because maybe they died in their sleep or maybe their priest couldn't get to the hospital quick enough to administer the sacrament of "last rites," which cleans away all your sins in one swoop.

Purgatory is like Limbo except for grown-ups. I had two tiny infant brothers who died of birth defects and went to Limbo — this happened between me and Beck — and I never even got to see them, but I will never forget sitting on my dad's lap when he broke the news to me that they wouldn't be coming home from the hospital with Mommy. Daddy kept hugging me and saying how much he loved me.

When you're in Purgatory, the only way you can finally fly into heaven is when people say enough prayers for you or pay to have enough masses said in your name. Nobody has ever given me a straight answer about how many actual prayers or masses are required. It's all very fuzzy. God must have a whole room full of angels keeping those numbers straight.

I say two more Hail Marys just in case my papa or Uncle Mark are still in purgatory. I highly doubt that though because we all pray for them and Nana buys a Mass in each of their names every month and on their birthdays. You can buy a "High Mass" or a "Low Mass." The high ones cost more and so I suppose they work better.

My father's in the confessional a long time, longer than usual. It's so quiet in here. Tomorrow these pews will be filled with people for Mass. We'll stand and sit and kneel together. We'll sing together, and say memorized prayers together, but the only person who can really talk, say what's on his mind, is Father Reilly. That can get boring.

A lady moves to the table by the votive candles where there's a silver box labeled INTENTIONS. It has a lock on it. There's a stack of small white slips of paper and short pencils. The lady writes something on a paper and sticks it in the box. She lights a candle and kneels down to pray. I asked my mother once, "Does Father Reilly read all those intentions?" and she said she didn't think so; they are meant for God.

I would like to read them. I would love to know what all these people are praying for. Maybe we could help one another out more if we knew what everybody wanted. God doesn't need to read those papers. God knows everything, right?

I look around at the stations of the cross and then the statues — Mary and Joseph and Michael with his angel wings — but I'm drawn, like always, to the face of Jesus nailed on the huge cross above the altar.

For once, I wish Jesus would just open his eyes, *just once*, so I could see him and he could see me, Aislinn O'Neill, and I could talk to him and tell him how hard it is living in the jailhouse with Dad's drinking getting worse and how I'm trying, really trying to make things better but nothing I do seems to work. . . .

Finally the confessional curtain moves and my dad comes out. He kneels back down next to me and bows his head, covering his whole face with his hands, saying whatever penance Father Reilly gave him. He prays for an extra long time today, making a whimpering sound and then sniffling.

When Dad finally looks up, his eyes are red from crying.

Good. Maybe this time he's truly "heartily sorry" for drinking so much and being so mean. Maybe this new baby coming will change things. Maybe instead of heading to the liquor store for his weekly supply of bottles like we usually do, we'll go straight home and Dad will take us out to the Red Front for pizza and then to Wilson's for ice cream and then we'll come home and play Monopoly and the phone will ring and Maizey will invite me for a sleepover and Dad will say, "Sure, go ahead, honey, have fun." Maybe this time confession worked.

When we walk outside into the sunshine, I look across the street to the Carrolls' house. Maria and Leo are holding hands, laughing, walking toward their car.

"Maria!" I shout across to her.

"Aislinn! Hello!"

Leo waves. "Hi, A." He nods. "Mr. O'Neill."

Dad gives a quick wave in return.

"How's college?" I shout.

"Great," Maria says. "Come visit us and I'll tell you all about it."

"Come on, monkey, let's go," Dad says.

Leo opens the car door for Maria and when she gets in he closes it. I see her slide across the front seat and push open the door for him. They are so nice to each other.

We get in our car. Dad looks relieved, happy. "Ready, monkey?"

"Yep!" I get in and buckle up, feeling hopeful.

Dad turns on the radio. It's a corny song he likes called "Tiny Bubbles" and he starts singing. "Come on," he says, "you know the words," and I join in like I always used to.

"Tiny bubbles in the wine. Make me happy. Make me feel fine . . ." My heart is feeling bubbly all right. Dad's car picks up speed. My hair's blowing back crazy in the

wind. Maybe I'll even ask him about going on vacation with Maizey's family. She asks me every summer, and I can never go. . . .

No! At the light Dad turns right, instead of left toward our house, and all the tiny bubbles *pop, pop, pop.* We head up the hill toward the liquor store. I cross my arms, angry, and zip my lips, sad, staring out the window. He keeps singing.

Dad shuts off the car in front of the store. "Coming in?" he says.

"No, thank you," I say, hoping the tone of my voice shows my disapproval.

When I was younger, I used to actually like going into this store with my dad. The owner was always glad to see us, smiling at Dad and holding out that big candy dish to me, "Go ahead, take a handful, honey."

Ugh. I'd like to spit at that man and his candy dish now.

How am I going to get my dad to stop drinking?

Nana can't help.

Confession doesn't work.

My mother . . . she hates that he drinks and she keeps trying to get him to stop, but she always forgives him. She keeps thinking it will get better, I guess, or that

God will take care of it. But she's our mother, our *mother.* She's supposed to protect us, right? I'm going to have to do this on my own. I know down deep my dad is good. He's still the dad I love. I know he must want to change. Why else would he keep going to confession every Saturday and Mass every Sunday?

A blue station wagon pulls up next to our car. It's Maizey's parents, Mr. and Mrs. Hogan. I slink down in my seat before they see me, embarrassed to be at a liquor store.

"Don't be a tightwad, John," Mrs. Hogan shouts out the window. "Get a nice bottle of wine. The Dandridges are classy people."

I sink lower in my seat, depressed. The Dandridges, that's Snoop-Melon's family, must have invited Maizey's parents to dinner. Maizey is probably already at their house. She and Snoop-Melon are probably having a sleepover with fancy canapés and ginger ale with straws. I bet the Snoop has a big beautiful color-coordinated room with frilly lace curtains and her own record player and posters of the Beatles and the Beach Boys and I'm sure she doesn't have to share it with anybody.

My parents never have friends over to dinner. No St. Patrick's Day parties like we had down in the basement long ago. Now that Papa and Uncle Mark are gone, Nana's the only one who comes for our birthdays and Sunday dinners. I could never figure out why Dad wouldn't let Mom invite relatives over to our house (I love *most* of my cousins) but now I know it's because Dad doesn't want anybody seeing him drink so much.

And maybe it's good no friends from school ever come to my house. After that fourth-grade nightmare, I've got enough to be ashamed about without adding "and your dad's a drunk" to the list. Maizey's the only one who knows.

But if nobody sees what's going on . . . how am I ever going to get help?

When Dad gets back in the car he puts the heavy brown paper bag full of bottles on the floor next to my feet. "Watch they don't break," he says. He turns on the radio, finds a Sinatra song he likes, and turns up the volume.

He checks out his reflection in the rearview mirror. He drives fast, too fast. Thank God he hasn't started drinking yet. I pull my seat belt tighter around me, holding my hair in a bunch to keep it from whipping against my eyes.

Dad brakes quickly at a red light and I jolt forward, my head nearly hitting the dashboard, the glass bottles clinking in the bag.

"I said watch them," Dad says, looking down at the bottles like they're fragile newborn chicks. He reaches over, opens the glove compartment, takes out a map, and hands it to me. "Here, wrap this in around them."

I unfold the map of New York State and weave it in between the bottles. I have studied this map before. As we drive home I imagine sneaking out of my room late tonight, after my father is out-cold drunk on the couch, and taking all of these bottles and cracking them open, *crack, crack, crack,* in the sink like one-two-three eggs for a birthday cake, then watching the brown liquid swirl down the drain where it can't ever hurt my family again. Then I'll grill four cheese sandwiches, fill a thermos with soda, sling my guitar on my back, open the map of New York and pick a city far away from Troy — past Albany, past Schenectady, past Utica, past Syracuse, past Rochester and Buffalo, maybe as far as Niagara Falls — and I'll head my bike in that direction.

See ya later, alligators. I'm the boss now, applesauce.

Prisoner Number One, Aislinn aka "Dream" O'Neill, has escaped the penitentiary.

CHAPTER EIGHT
A Most Exciting Saturday Night

We are the music-makers
And we are the dreamers of dreams . . .
— Arthur William Edgar O'Shaughnessy

When Dad and I get home, he pours a drink in the kitchen and shouts to my mother, who is in their bedroom getting dressed. "Maggie, are you ready yet?"

"Be there in a sec, Roe," she calls back.

My parents are going out to dinner like they do every Saturday night, even though we are saving for a house, even though my mother is nauseated from being pregnant, even though my father shouldn't drive when he's drinking.

"Order a pizza, Aislinn," Dad says to me. "I'll go pick it up."

Callie claps her hands and runs to tell Beck the good news.

Big deal, a pizza, who cares. I call the Red Front and order a large cheese pizza with sausage and mushrooms. Hopefully it will be ready when my father gets there and he won't go to the bar while he's waiting.

In my parents' room, Mom is rolling pink sponge curlers into her hair. She's wearing a long purple dress. "I had to get the tents back out," she says to me, smiling, referring to her maternity clothes. "And I was doing so well on my diet again."

Mom doesn't look happy about going out to dinner. She looks tired, sad. I know she doesn't like leaving us. I know she feels guilty about me having to babysit all the time. I know she worries about my father drinking and driving, but she goes along with it all to "keep the peace."

"Let us offer each other a sign of peace," Father Reilly says at Sunday Mass now, it's a new thing that the pope ordered, and we shake everyone's hands in the pews around us saying, "Peace be with you" . . . "peace be with you" . . . "peace be with you."

"Hey, Frisky, peace be with you." I lift Frisky into a pan, then go dump the stinky water out of his pool house, wipe it out, and refill it with fresh water. I plop him back in and shake in some turtle food flakes for dinner. Frisky swims around his palm tree and then crawls across his little bridge. I put my face real close to him so we can see eye to eye. He blinks. I touch his shell. "I wish you could talk."

My father is gone for forty-five minutes. When he comes back he's carrying the box of pizza and a tray of Hot Dog Charlie's — miniature hot dogs in little rolls smothered in meat sauce — and a bag of treats: orange soda and onion-garlic potato chips and Freihofer's chocolate chip cookies.

He lines all the stuff on the counter like a display. "Everything you like, A, right?" he says to me with a nod, expecting me to be all happy. I shrug and turn away. I'd rather have the money for a bathing suit. I'd rather be the one going out tonight with my friends. I wonder what Maizey's doing? I wonder what Mike's doing?

I put a slice of pizza and one hot dog on each plate. I fold paper napkins and pour milk. "Come on, everybody, dinner's ready," I call.

B, C, D, and I take our usual places around the gray-white speckled formica table with the old Christmas card folded under the left corner leg because it lost its little rubber bottom thingy and it's shorter than the other legs now.

My father looks up at the clock and huffs. "Come on, Mags, I'm starving," he shouts to my mother. "What the heck you doing in there? You're slow as mule, let's go!"

Mule, how mean. My mother is not. I lock eyes with Callie. I watch my father pour another drink. He takes out a chunk of cheddar cheese, opens a box of Ritz crackers, slices the cheese with a sharp knife.

"Whatcha gonna put in our grilled cheese next time?" Beck asks me, trying admirably to make dinner conversation.

"I don't know," I say. "Any ideas?"

"How 'bout hot dogs?" Dooley suggests, and Callie giggles.

"What?" Dooley says, looking hurt. "That'd taste good."

I watch my father put mustard on his crackers and cheese. I probably got the cheese gene from him, but no way am I ever making him one of my famous sandwiches.

My mom comes into the kitchen, smelling of her favorite cherry-almond Jergens lotion. Her hair looks fancy; she's wearing lipstick. Her eyes take in all the food treats, the glass in my father's hand, the newly opened liquor bottle, how much is already gone.

My father finishes his drink. "Okay, finally, let's go," he says, putting the cheese back in the refrigerator, not saying my mother looks nice or anything.

"Your hair looks pretty, Mommy," Callie says.

"Thanks, honey," she says.

"I like your red lips," Callie says.

My mother smiles.

"Where are you going to dinner?" I ask.

"Villa Valenti," Dad says. "Come on, Mags. I'll meet you in the car." And he's off out the door.

My mother touches her stomach.

"Are you feeling okay?" I ask. She nods and gives me a look like "don't mention the baby." I bet she doesn't want to get the little ones all excited because then they'll be asking "when it's coming?" every day for the next five months and of course there's always the chance something will go wrong. She wasn't supposed to have any more.

Mom kisses B, D, and C on their foreheads, rests her hand on Eddie's head.

"We should be home by eleven," she says to me.

The car horn *beep-beep-beeps* down in the driveway.

My mother sighs. "Be good for A," she says.

After dinner, I clean up, then sweep the kitchen floor, twice, not a crumb in sight, and then put the broom and dustpan in the corner by the pantry.

"Can we have a show, A?" Beck asks.

"Sure, why not," I say.

"Yeah!" he yells, running to get the others.

"Come on, big guy," I say, to Eddie. "You are such a porky pudge ball." I change him then put him in his high chair. I heat up his turkey noodle vegetable baby food jar in a pan of water on the stove. I feed him applesauce for dessert.

B, C, and D line up on the couch, front row seats. I prop Eddie on the end.

I strum my guitar and adjust a string.

"Do 'Raindrops'!" Callie shouts, my first audience request.

"Okay," I say, starting out with "Raindrops Keep Fallin' on My Head" by B. J. Thomas and then "We've Only Just Begun" by the Carpenters and "Bridge Over Troubled Water" by Simon & Garfunkel.

"Do 'Proud Mary'!" Beck shouts and I nod, happy to keep my fans happy.

When I start belting out "Proud Mary" by Creedence Clearwater Revival, B, C, and D stand up on the couch, rocking their hips, and rolling their hands, singing *"Rollin! . . . Rollin! . . . Rollin on a river."* Eddie kneels and claps.

"You are excellent backup singers," I say, applauding for them. "We could've been on *The Ed Sullivan Show!*" Beck pushes his fist up in victory, and they all plop back down on the couch, giggling. Dooley hugs Eddie.

When it's time for intermission, I put out the treats Dad bought — Wise onion-garlic potato chips, my favorite orange soda, and Freihofer's chocolate chip cookies.

"Not too many," I tell Dooley as he reaches for another fist of the little round tan cookies the size of silver dollars. "You don't want to get a tummy-ache."

For my second act I sing "I'll Be There" and "ABC" by the Jackson Five — I love their music (Michael's my favorite) — and then move on to some Beatles songs, finishing up with "Let It Be."

"Okay, ladies and gentlemen, the show is over, time for bed. Brush your teeth and go pee," I tell Beck and Callie. I make Dooley sit on his potty, "You're a big boy now," then help him into his race car pajamas.

We say our prayers. "Now I lay me down to sleep, I pray the Lord my soul to keep, if I should die before I wake, I pray the Lord my soul to take. God bless Mommy and Daddy and Nana, and Papa and Uncle Mark in heaven, Amen."

I make sure all the little ones have their favorite luvies snug in their arms, Dooley's got his favorite red Matchbox, too, and then I kiss them, "Sweet dreams."

It's nine o'clock on a Saturday night. Now what?

I kneel on the couch in my father's favorite spot, looking down at the cars going by. There's a bit of a breeze through the screen, good thing. The windowsill needs a cleaning. A fly buzzes, head *bang-bang*ing against the screen, trying to get out. A plane roars by overhead. I think about Nana out in California. "I'm leaving on a jet plane, don't know when I'll be back again . . ." my favorite Peter, Paul and Mary song.

I go into my dad's office. On his desk is the rock paperweight with "Best Dad" painted on it that I gave him for Father's Day years ago, his customer order pad, a can of pens, a calendar, the packet of HELLO MY NAME IS labels.

Bored, bored, bored. I pour another glass of orange soda, eat another piece of pizza. In my bedroom I lift the bottom corner of my mattress and pull out my pink, yellow, and orange flowered diary, with the nearly cracked spine and the frayed gold ribbon that marks my spot, and then I take out the key from Jeffrey's pocket and unlock the little gold clasp.

Callie mumbles in her sleep, *hope it's a happy dream*, her body snuggled toward the yellow plaster wall. I turn on my desk lamp, move the arm so an O of light shines just on my desk, and I sit down and begin to write.

Dear Diary,

So much to tell you. Where do I begin?

I saw Mike Mancinello, who I'll just call MM from now on, and he said hello to me! He is sooooo cute. I've known him my whole life but this is only the second time we really talked. The first was the last day of school when he said I could sit with him on the bus. If that doesn't mean something, I don't know what does!

It hurt seeing Maizey and Snoop-Melon going to the country club. Please, God, don't let her take Maizey away from me. Maizey is my best friend.

Oh well, that's all for now.

A

Callie laughs in her dream, *good*, and rolls over in her bunk. I lock my diary, stuff it back under the mattress, and put the key back in Jeffrey's pocket.

It's nine thirty. Now what?

I turn on the television and check out the three channels. A detective show, an old war movie, a comedy that isn't making me laugh.

My parents' bedroom is off the living room. A little snooping might be fun. I open the top drawer of my mother's dresser and fish around to see if there's anything in there besides bras and slips and rubber girdles.

Sure enough, there's a book stuffed way back in the right-hand corner. I pull it out. On the cover is a handsome dark-haired man kissing a beautiful woman in a red gown. I open the book and leaf through the pages, read a few lines. Ooh, *sexy*, as Maizey would say. I close the book and put it back where it was. Next, I check out the far back left-hand corner. Gold again. There's a black oblong-shaped case like you would keep eyeglasses in, except my mother doesn't wear glasses. I open it.

Cigarettes! Four long white ones and a few that have burnt tips like they were smoked a bit and then saved and a pack of matches from a restaurant called Dino's where we go sometimes on very special occasions and I order baked scallops because I think "scallops" sounds so romantic.

I read the brand name on one of the cigarettes. "Salem." I take a whiff. *Eeew.*

My mother reads romance novels?

My mother smokes cigarettes?

Well, I'll be a monkey's uncle.

The phone rings. I snap the case shut, stuff it back where it was, close the drawer, and run to the phone in the dining room. *Finally, Maizey.*

"Hello?"

"Hi. . . . . .A?

It's a boy!

"It's me, Mike. . . . . .Mancinello."

Boom, boom, boom, boom, boom, my heart pounds like a drum.

"I hope it was okay to call you," he says.

"Sure," I say. "That's fine."

"What are you doing?" he says.

"Nothing much," I say, perching my butt on the armrest of the phone bench, feet on the seat, looking out the window, where I can quickly spot my father's car if it pulls in the driveway. They won't be home for a while yet. I can talk as long as I want. I feel a wave of happiness, *free*.

"What are you doing?" I say.

"Talking to you," he says.

We laugh.

Finally, we think of some things to talk about. Television shows mostly. We talk for twenty-two minutes. I time it on my watch.

When we say good-bye I run and pull my diary out again.

> *PS My mother smokes and reads sexy*
> *novels. And MM called me!!!!!!!!! Who*
> *knew Saturday night could be such fun!!!*

At eleven thirty I get into bed. This isn't good that they aren't home yet. By now my father is probably mumbling his words and stumbling when he walks. My mother is trying to reason with him. "Come on, Roe, give me the keys."

Tomorrow we will all parade up the hill and into church like the perfect family. After dinner we'll probably go for a ride to see our house. *Oh, please let tomorrow be the Sunday it finally truly becomes "ours."*

I think about going to confession with my father, seeing that lady write her wish on a slip of paper and put it in that silver box. Oh, if it was only that easy to make a dream come true . . . just write it on a slip of paper like that.

People should share their dreams with other people, not hide them in a box.

I sit up in bed.

I think of Dad's labels. HELLO MY NAME IS . . . *Maybe people should write their dreams on stickers like that and wear them right on their sleeves for the whole world to see. Who knows . . . maybe the person you pass on the street or shake hands with, "peace be with you," might be the exact perfect person to help you make your wish come true.*

People should wear their dreams on their sleeves.

Yes! My body is shaking. I turn on the light, get my diary back out.

"Dreamsleeves," I write and stare at the word.

Dreamsleeves.

I smile. I like the sound of it.

"Dreamsleeves, Dreamsleeves, Dreamsleeves."

Now what will I do with that?

CHAPTER NINE
The Peely-Stick Shop

God's gifts put man's best dreams to shame.
— ELIZABETH BARRETT BROWNING

Sunday morning I wake to the sound of my father puking in the bathroom. There's a pause, then more awful retching.

I almost feel sorry for him.

They came in late last night, him shouting, my mother pleading with him to be quiet. "Shut up," he said to her, "go to bed." Then it was quiet. After a while, I peeked out my door. He was asleep on the living room couch.

Back in bed, I held Flop, and then Jeffrey, and then my doll, Clarissa, tight, taking turns so no one got left out, lying awake for a long time listening, listening to make sure he was out for good.

The next morning, in our Sunday best, we walk up

the hill to church, Dad leading the way with Mom beside him pushing Eddie in his stroller, then me holding Dooley's hand, then Beck and Callie side by side. There's the old man in the brown suit and matching hat with the gray feather, almost looks like a seagull feather, hunched over praying. We pass by Maria and Leo Carroll. Maria reaches out to touch my arm and winks.

We take our usual place up in the front right-hand corner. As we stand for the opening hymn, "Number 308," I hear shuffling in the pew behind us as latecomers take a seat, and I turn around to look.

Mike Mancinello! And that's probably his mother and father! I didn't know they belonged to this church. Mike smiles at me and I smile back, heart pounding. I swerve back around, hoping my father doesn't notice.

When we get to the Sign of Peace, thank goodness for this new part, Mike shakes my hand a bit longer then he should and I have to stifle a giggle. I shake his mom's hand and his dad's. I don't dare look my father's way.

"Who was that boy in church, Aislinn?" Dad says to me when we get home.

"What boy?"

"That Italian one behind us."

I hate that my father said that. Why does he always have to make such a big deal over whether's somebody's Italian or Polish. We're all American, right?

"No boys, Aislinn," my father squints at me, finger pointing. "Do you hear me? No daughter of mine's going to go running around like some . . ."

"Roe, *stop*," my mother says.

"I mean it," my father says to me. "No boys till you're seventeen."

"Seventeen!" I say, my voice screeching. "You said high school, Dad. I'll be graduating by the time I'm seventeen. . . ." But he's off, slamming the door behind him.

"*Seventeen?* Mom . . . come on!" Angry tears fill my eyes. My mother looks ghost pale, like she's going to be sick, so I don't argue with her. It wouldn't do any good anyway. She never stands up to him. Seventeen? That's so unfair. It's criminal. He has no right to treat me like this. I didn't do anything wrong! All I did was shake a boy's hand, in church even, and it's part of the Mass, the pope said so!

Later, when the little ones are napping, I escape up to the top of the hill to my Peely-Stick Shop. This is my house. I lay back on the soft mossy ground and stare up at the tiny sun-stars blinking in through the pine boughs and let the tears come.

I just want to have a normal summer ... go places with my friends ... the park, the town pool, the movies ... Is that too much to ask?

I think about Dreamsleeves ... the cool idea I had last night. Now it just seems stupid. Who'd ever want to help me anyway?

I'm nobody. Just Aislinn O'Neill, a monkey-scrawny girl living in a jailhouse with a father who drinks and a mouse-afraid mother who won't make him stop and too many babies all in a row ... a girl so nervous about listening to make sure everyone's safe at night that sometimes she wets the bed and wakes up smelling like pee in the morning and can't get in the one bathroom to wash before school because her father's got the door locked throwing up again with his "weak stomach" which is really the liquor from the night before gurgling up in his throat like a sewer and it was on one of those days in fourth grade that she couldn't get in the bathroom that the new girl, Sue-Ellen Dandridge, pretty as Miss America comes to class and Sister Mary Alice seats her right behind me and an hour later the new girl starts *sniff-sniff*ing the air around my back and says, "Oh my god, she smells like pee!" loud enough for the whole class to hear.

In that moment when Sue-Ellen said that and the whole room clouded dark and I thought I'd faint from embarrassment, I could hear my mother's voice in my head, "Jesus suffered and died on the cross for us, Aislinn. Can't you bear this little burden for him? Just offer it up to Jesus." And I thought I to myself, *no, sorry, I can't. I hate that girl.*

A bird chatters and another answers. I wipe my face and look around my Peely-Stick Shop, breathing in the pine scent, squeezing a tiny pinecone in my hand. "This too shall pass," I tell myself. That's another thing my mother always says.

My Peely-Stick Shop is a circle of birch trees — tall, thin white trunks with black patches — like the Dalmatian dog version of trees. There's a huge old pine tree beside them with thick green boughs that have spread over the tops of the birches to make a roof, thick enough to keep the rain out most days, with just a few spots to let sun drops in.

The Peely-Stick Shop is mine, just mine. Intruders would have to hike through overgrown masses of pricker-bushes to get here unless they knew about the secret path

I cleared with a weed-whacker and gardening gloves and lots of sweaty hard work. I had blisters on my hands and cuts up and down my legs and prickers stuck to my socks and sneaker laces, but it was worth it.

I think if there's someplace you really need to go, you have to make your own path, because nobody else is going to do it for you.

I call the birch trees "peely-sticks" because they are skinny as sticks and their bark peels off in patches. Mom told me the Native American Indians used to etch words and pictures on the birch peels to tell stories and pass along messages.

I can't imagine how you'd fit a whole story on a peely-stick page, but I etch happy words like *Smile* and *Sing* and I hang them inside my shop. I use thumbtacks so I don't hurt the trees. So far they haven't complained.

I call this place my "shop" because I make presents here — birthday and holiday gifts for my family. Little stick dolls for Callie; wildflower bouquets for Nana and Mom that I tie with ribbons and hang from a rope clothesline to dry; and paperweights — smooth rocks that I clean off and paint messages on. Mom uses the "Believe" paperweight I gave her for her birthday to keep her GANE papers in order when she writes. Dad keeps his "Best Dad" rock on his desk. I'd never give him a present like that anymore.

When I first discovered this circle of birches about five years ago, I thought somebody must have planted these trees to grow up so perfectly to make this round house with the pine roof that smelled so beautiful.

When year after year no one else came to claim it, I figured God built it for me. God knew just what Aislinn O'Neill needed and sent it as a present just for me.

A place where I could be A.

I wish everybody in the world could have a peely-stick shop sort of place. It doesn't have to be fancy, big or small, indoors or outdoors, it doesn't matter. It just has to be a place you can call your own — a place where you can dream.

When I leave for college to be a teacher, I'm going to pass on my Peely-Stick Shop to Callie. She will love it. And then maybe someday, she'll pass it on to Dool or Eddie or the new baby on the way.

After college I will marry a handsome boy like Mike Mancinello and we'll be so happy together like Maria and Leo Carroll. We'll have breakfast each morning, jelly donuts and tea, and he'll kiss me good-bye and go to work and I'll head off to teach my class. Fifth grade, I think, or maybe fourth.

Dreamsleeves.

Maybe the most important dreams we have are connected to our particular gifts, the talents we are born with that we are somehow meant to share. I'm pretty sure that that my gift is teaching. I want to do for other people what my fifth-grade teacher, Miss McMahon, did for me — to create a class space that feels safe and encouraging, to take the time to really pay attention to my students and help them discover their talents — to inspire them and believe in them and help them stand *"up, up with people."*

Twisting the top off the jar of bubbles I always keep in my shop, I dip the wand in and blow a huge bubble skyward, smiling as the sun paints it red, yellow, blue.

Thank you, God, for my Peely-Stick Shop. You can't put a dream on your sleeve to come true if you don't know what your dream is, right? And I might never have discovered what my particular talent is if I didn't have a place of my own, quiet enough to close my eyes and listen, really listen so I could hear my dream and pull it up . . . up, up out of my heart.

CHAPTER TEN
The Invitation

She . . . trembled to think of
that mysterious thing in the soul,
which seems to acknowledge no human jurisdiction,
but in spite of the individual's own innocent self,
will still dream . . .
— HERMAN MELVILLE

hird time for Tommy Doyle," my father says to no one in particular as I come out into the kitchen Monday morning. He has the newspaper open on the table. When he looks up, I see that his eyes are wet with tears.

I walk to the table to look. It's an obituary notice. The wake is tomorrow at Clinton Funeral Home. That's where my uncle Mark's wake was. "I'm sorry, Dad."

"Tommy Doyle was a good one," Dad says. "Say a

prayer for him, A." He blows his nose on a white hand-kerchief and sticks it back in his pocket. "Let me tell you something, A, there's three times you get your name in the paper — when you're born, when you're married, and when you die. But there's only *one time* they'll stop traffic for you."

"When's that, Dad?"

"When you die."

My mind flashes back to my uncle Mark's funeral, how we drove in a rented black Cadillac behind the hearse carrying his coffin and how we went straight through red lights at all of the intersections, halting traffic all the way to St. Mary's Cemetery. Nana's friends from the Women's Guild sent covered dishes for a luncheon at Nana's afterward. Maria Carroll brought down a tray of lasagna and three dozen sugar cookies. I miss my uncle Mark. He loved me.

"I'm sorry, Dad." I reach out to touch his shoulder.

He refolds the paper, sniffs, and stands. "Gotta go, monkey," he says, nodding at the clock. "Time is money and I'm broke."

At the door he turns back around. "How about we go to Hoffman's tonight? We haven't been there in ages."

Hoffman's Playland. My dad and I love the fast rides,

the faster the better, the roller coaster and the Scrambler. We go every summer. Just us two. I wish I could go there with Mike.

"Sure, Dad." I try to sound happy. "That'd be great."

"All right then," he says. "Get that laundry done today, will you?"

I take my class on a field trip walk up behind the outhouse, near the swing set. I teach them the names of the flowers, just like my mom taught me — white Queen Anne's lace, blue cornflowers, yellow buttercups, purple thistles — it's a good way to teach Dooley and Eddie their colors, too. I point out wild strawberries almost ready to pick and some other round, shiny red berries. "Don't ever, *ever* touch these. They are poisonous."

Back in our classroom, we do art, coloring pictures of the flowers we saw. I tape their pictures up so they dangle down from the hubcaps. "You are Picassos and Michelangelos," I say, "Monets and Degases."

Beck and Callie giggle at the sounds of these foreign names. Eddie peels the wrapper from a purple crayon. "No, Eddie," Dooley says, taking it away from him.

When I walk down to the mailbox that afternoon, Eddie in my arms and Dooley nearly tripping me when he bends to retrieve one of his Matchbox race cars, there is something spectacular in the mailbox.

A letter for me?

No. Something better.

An invitation!

Sue-Ellen Dandridge is having a thirteenth birthday party. *Oh, why does it have to be her?* A pool party at her parent's club, the Valleyview Country Club, on Saturday, July 24, from two until five P.M. "Hot Dogs and Hamburgers will be served. And cake and ice cream, of course! Wear a suit and bring a towel. RSVP by July 18 to Mrs. Rodney Dandridge III at ASH-4745."

My heart is pounding. *Oh, how I'd love to go to a pool party. But Snoop-Melon? Ugh . . . Why does it have to be that girl? Not that my father will let me go anyway.* Eddie tries to pull the invitation from my hand.

"No!" I shout too loudly. His lips pucker, about to cry.

"Sorry, E," I say, kissing his fat cheek. "It's mine."

The telephone's ringing upstairs.

"Go, go, go," Dooley shouts, and sends his favorite red Matchbox car zooming down the sloped concrete walkway that runs along the side of our house.

"Come on, Dooley," I say, reaching for his hand. "The phone."

"Wait," he says, watching his car race away, his face all lit up excited.

The little red car grows smaller and smaller as it races down the hill then vaults off the top step of the staircase that leads to the sidewalk and road below and is gone. The phone keeps ringing. D pulls my hand. "Come on, A. Let's get it!"

"No, D, the phone." *It might be Mike or Maizey.* "I'll get your car later. Come on!" I take his hand and yank him along, him crying and protesting.

I rush up the steps, across the porch, and into the house, plunk Eddie into his crib, and then pick up the receiver. D and E are both crying now.

"A! It's me."

Maizey. Finally. Maybe she's coming over.

"Guess what?" she says.

"What?" I say, panting and sweating, trying to catch my breath.

"Sue-Ellen's parents are inviting our whole class to *a boy-girl birthday party*, at their country club, which is absolutely beautiful, let me tell you. Isn't that something?"

"Yes," I say. "I just got my invitation." B and C are giggling in the living room, still side by side on the couch, watching the TV show I turned on for them before I went down to get the mail.

"Don't worry," Maizey says. "We'll make up something."

The "we" makes me feel good. Maizey means we will have to think up a story so that my dad will let me go to the party. If he hears that boys are invited, he won't let me go. My heart is pounding. Maybe Mike will be there. I have to go! But I don't have a decent bathing suit. And what if my father got suspicious and followed me to the party? He started checking up on me like that last year after one of his drinking buddies said, "You're gonna have to lock that one up, Roe. She's gonna be a looker like her mother."

That stupid, drunk old jerk. Why did he have to make my life even harder than it was by saying that? I looked in the bathroom mirror and studied my face that night. I didn't see what he was talking about. I looked the same as I always do.

Last year the Keating twins up on Stowe Avenue invited me and Maizey to a double date matinee at Proctors. The Keating twins have been our friends since kindergarten, we all wait at the same bus stop together, so it didn't even seem like a real boy-girl date or anything. Maizey's father was going to drive the four of us and pick us up right after the movie. My mom said I could go, but "just don't tell your father."

Even though Jackie Keating had really bad breath and he didn't even try to hold my hand, it was an okay first not-real-date, I guess. But as I ate buttery popcorn and sipped cola, I couldn't focus on the movie I was so nervous . . . what if my father found out?

Sure enough, when the four of us walked out into the sunshine from the dark theater, waiting for Mr. Hogan's car, eating the stash of candy Mrs. Keating sent for us to eat, my heart froze when I saw my father's car pull up.

He leaned across the front seat and yelled out the window. "Get in!"

My whole body turned red with shame and my legs wobbled with fear as I walked to the car. Tires squealed as we pulled away. He drove fast and yelled, but he didn't hit me, probably because it was a Sunday. "You're grounded," he shouted when we got home, which was a meaningless punishment because I can never go anywhere anyway. Then late that night he banged on my door with a broom in his hand. "Get out there and sweep the dining room."

But what if . . . just maybe . . . I can go to the pool party. Imagine spending all that time, three whole hours, with Mike.

Dooley is still crying about his red car.

"Okay, okay. I'll go get it. Stay here."

I head down past the mailbox, following the path the little red Matchbox took. It's not on the front steps, not on the sidewalk. I look out on the road, cars whizzing past.

I see something red way over against the far curb, but it's tiny as a measle. It could be anything, really. And there is absolutely no way to investigate except to cross four lanes of traffic, which is definitely not going to happen.

When I come back empty-handed, Dooley cries even harder. "But that's my best one!" he says. He runs to the couch in the living room and looks out the window, down toward the road, his forehead pushing against the thin screen.

"Don't do that, D!" I say. "You'll fall out and kill yourself."

"Please, A, please," he cries. "I see it. There it is!"

I kneel next to him and put my arm around him. I stare down but I don't see even the measle anymore. "I'm sorry, Dool, but it's gone. You've got lots of others."

"No!" he says. "Please, A, go find it."

"Your blue car's really sharp, buddy. And the black Corvette. I love that one."

"But the red's my favorite," he screams. "It's just like Daddy's." He runs to his bunk and cries as if he's lost his very best friend.

After lunch, grilled cheese with cut-up green grapes on top, I read B and C three Curious George books on the couch and send them to their beds for "quiet time." I put D down for a nap. He turns away so I can't kiss his cheek.

"I'm sorry, Dool. I'll get you a new red one for your birthday."

"But I want that one, A, *that one*." He kicks the wall. "It's my best one."

"I know, honey, I'm sorry."

Sitting in my mother's chair, rocking E to sleep, I think about how much I hate Sue-Ellen for saying I smelled like pee in fourth grade, but how nice it would be to go to a pool party. I close my eyes and picture myself at a fancy country club like I've seen on TV, climbing to the top of the diving board, sashaying across it like a model, arching into a perfect dive, slipping into the water smooth as satin, with not so much as a splash.

When I surface, Mike Mancinello is leaning over the edge of the pool, looking down at me, smiling, with those gorgeous brown eyes. "Need a lift, A?" he says.

I hold out my hand, pretty pink manicured nails and all. "Sure, thanks," I say, flipping my wet hair back off my shoulder, all casual, and he pulls me out of the pool.

Mike offers me his towel and I dry off and we go to get cheeseburgers and all the other girls are watching us, jealous because he is the cutest boy ever. And then Snoop-Melon trips in the pool and drowns — *no, sorry, God, erase that* — she just slips in the pool and gulps in too much chlorine and it makes her throw up and snort bubbles out of her nose. I walk over to her, all make-believe concerned, hand in hand with Mike, and then I lean down and I *sniff, sniff, sniff* around her face.

"Oh my gosh, everybody," I shout, "she smells like puke!"

CHAPTER ELEVEN
The Betrayal

Nothing happens unless first a dream.

— CARL SANDBURG

I decide to test out my Dreamsleeves idea with a small but important wish. I take one of the Hello labels from my father's desk. Last year my dad won "most humorous" speech at one of his meetings. People say my dad is such a funny guy. There's a picture of him on the wall. He looks maybe seventeen. He's lying on his back on the roof of a car, his arms making a pillow behind his neck, gazing up at the sky. It's summer, just before dark. My dad is smiling. He looks happy.

In my room I cut the HELLO MY NAME IS part off the label. I print *New Bathing Suit* on the white space, peel off the backing, and stick my dream on my T-shirt sleeve, up top, facing out.

When my mother gets home from work, she slumps down on a kitchen chair. Her ankles are swollen and her face is flushed and sweaty from the heat.

"Get me a Tab and some chips, will you, A?" she says.

"Sure, Mom."

She takes a long drink of soda and eats some potato chips. I get the portable fan from the living room and plug it in so it faces her.

"Thanks, honey," she says, "you're so thoughtful."

She closes her eyes and I stand there in front of her watching the breeze blow wisps of damp brown hair from her face.

Finally, after a while, she opens her eyes. She sees the dream on my sleeve. "What's that?" she says.

"I need a new bathing suit, Mom. Last year's is way too small for me."

"Okay. We can go pick out a pattern at Woolworth's Saturday."

I sigh, no. That's not what I had in mind.

My mother makes a lot of our clothes on her Singer sewing machine in the dining room. When I was younger it was fun going to Woolworth's with her and picking out patterns for a sundress or a Halloween costume. But

I'm a teenager now! I don't want some babyish bathing suit with strawberries and a big poofy ruffle across the chest like last year. I would die of mortification wearing a bathing suit like that to Sue-Ellen's country club party. I'm sure Sue-Ellen orders her clothes from Sears.

Mom and I turn our heads at the sound of footsteps on the porch. The knob turns, the kitchen door opens. Dad's home. He's dressed in a light blue jacket, white shirt, striped tie, and gray pants. My dad always dresses like a million bucks. His fake Coppertone tan is looking a bit orange, and he's got a potbelly and is losing hair on the top of his head, but he's still handsome.

As he moves past me I smell his Old Spice Cologne and the cinnamon Dentyne gum he's always chewing. Dad walks straight to the cupboard and takes out a glass. He opens the freezer, crack-twists some ice cubes out of the tray. They tinkle as they slide into the glass. He opens a liquor bottle, almost empty although he just opened it new on Saturday night. He fills his glass nearly to the top, and then splashes in some ginger ale.

My mother watches all of this without a comment. She used to tell him to be careful, not to drink so much because of his stomach ulcer — his doctor warned him it was getting bad — but that just made my father angry and end up drinking more, so she doesn't nag him about it anymore. She eats another potato chip. She keeps the peace.

"What's for dinner?" Dad asks to no one in particular. His eyes rest on the potato chip bowl and he scowls at my mother. He's always saying sarcastic things to her about her weight. My mom is forever trying some new diet, but now that she's pregnant again, she can't go on a diet even if she wanted to. Now she has to eat for the baby, too.

"Hamburgers," Mom says.

"Again?" he says. "Don't make me one. I'll find something." Dad hardly ever joins us for dinner anymore. He prefers to eat alone, with a drink, in front of the TV in the living room.

Beck comes into the kitchen wearing his favorite Yankees cap.

"Hey, buster," Dad says to him, turning the cap so the lid's facing back.

Beck glows with the attention.

I move closer so Dad will see my dream.

"What's that?" Dad says, taking the bait.

Beck moves in to look. "What's it say?" he asks my mom.

She reads it for him.

Beck looks at me and smiles, interested.

A little white lie pops up like a spring crocus from the mud in Nana's garden. "I was thinking about how we're going to Uncle Tommy and Aunt Flo's camp pretty soon, Dad, and how all my girl cousins will be there, too, and how they always have brand-new bathing suits from . . ."

"Buy your daughter a bathing suit, will you?" Dad says to Mom in a mean voice. He takes another sip of his drink and nods disgustedly at the potato chip bowl. "And lay off the junk food, will you? You're breaking the scales as it is."

"I told A we'd pick out a pattern," Mom says, quietly. "We can go Saturday."

My dad takes a drink and then sneers at my mother. "I don't want my kids looking like hoboes at my brother's house again this year. Don't embarrass me again, Maggie. I work hard for this family, I bring in a good salary, the least you can do is dress these kids right."

Mom works hard, too, I shout inside myself. *And she has two jobs! Taking care of this family* and *working full-time. When you come home from work, you relax. Poor Mom comes home from work and has to cook dinner and . . .*

"And buy yourself some decent clothes when you take her shopping," Dad says, his eyes looking from Mom's swollen feet to her faded print blouse. "Flo always looks so sharp."

That's 'cause Aunt Flo doesn't have to work, I want to yell at him. *She has lots of time to flip through fashion magazines and get all the new hairstyles and clothes. . . .*

And I'm about to speak my mind to my father, sticking up for my mother now when it's still safe, before the drinks seep in and the mad sets in, when a little voice inside me shouts, "No! You're going to get a new bathing suit!" and I don't say a word.

I betray my mother for a bathing suit.

After dinner, Dad says to me, "Ready to go, monkey?"

We drive to Hoffman's Playland. I didn't want to go, but now I'm in a hopeful mood. I'm going to get a new bathing suit for the party! And besides, I feel bad that Dad's friend died and he has to go to his wake tomorrow.

At the amusement park, people are loading onto the little train at the stop.

Dad buys the ticket book with the least amount of rides. "Which first?" he says.

"Bumper cars," I say. And, *surprise*, when I stand back against the clown-faced measuring board, I'm finally tall enough to drive one by myself.

I choose a blue car. Dad chooses red. The race starts. I get rammed from behind. It's a boy a few years older than me. I hear a laugh and then a girl with long black hair rams into him. "Gotcha!" she shouts and he swerves off after her, smiling.

"Here I come!" he says. She laughs. They are probably a couple, on a date. I wish I could come here with Mike.

The little train chugs by and heads under the tunnel. People shout "ooh-ooh" like it's scary in that short stretch of dark before the train comes out the other side.

At the Ferris wheel, I quick climb into a seat and pull the bar locked. "I want to ride alone," I say.

"Oh, okay," my dad says, looking hurt. He gets in the cart behind me. I feel bad. I didn't mean to hurt his feelings. I just wanted to try it out alone for once.

When the ride's over, Dad says, "Scrambler, monkey?"

"Sure!" I say. This is the Dad I used to know. This is the Dad that's fun.

We climb into a seat together and he pulls the door closed tight. He nudges my elbow and smiles at me. "Ready?" he says with excitement.

This was always our favorite ride.

"Yep," I say, enjoying this, too.

The music starts up and we're off, whizzing forward, then zigzaggy side to side, my hair blowing wild in my face. "Woo-hoo!" Dad shouts and we laugh.

The tickets are done. "Ice cream?" he asks.

I glance at a little girl with blond curls pumping up and down on a merry-go-round horse, her father standing guard by her side. I remember how important it was to get the right horse. How high up I felt on that saddle. How fast we rode. How safe I felt with my daddy by my side.

Not anymore, no. Tonight was just him trying to get back on my good side after saying I couldn't date till I was seventeen. Tonight was just a fairy tale.

"Aislinn . . . I said do you want some ice cream?"

"No, thanks."

"Cotton candy?"

"No."

"You all right?" he says.

"I'm fine," I say.

We walk to the car and head home. We drive past a row of beautiful houses. Something catches my eye on the road up ahead.

It's a hubcap.

I look quick at my father. His gaze is straight ahead, lost in thought. He doesn't see the hubcap.

I don't point it out.

Lying in bed that night, looking up at the chicken-wire frame of Callie's bunk above me, I feel bad I didn't tell Dad about the hubcap, but no way as guilty as I feel for betraying my mom. I'm sorry, though. I need a new bathing suit and besides, I'm sick of defending my mother. She's supposed to look out for me, right? I'm done taking care of her. She's the mother; I'm the daughter. It's high time she realized that.

Just before I fall asleep, hugging my elf, Jeffrey, I think to myself, good for you, A. You tested out your idea. Dreamsleeves works! I bat Jeffrey's green cap and the little brass bell on the top jingles.

I can tell he's happy for me.

CHAPTER TWELVE
The Bathing Suit

If one advances confidently in the direction of his dreams,
and endeavors to live the life he has imagined,
he will meet with a success unexpected in common hours.
— HENRY DAVID THOREAU

On Saturday morning Mom and I drive to Two Guys for a bathing suit. I don't complain about why we're not going to Sears or Montgomery Ward. I'm sure I'll find something nice here.

"Hurry back," my dad says as we leave. He doesn't like having to watch all the little ones by himself. It's morning and he's not drinking yet, so I don't worry too much about him losing his temper with B, C, D, and E while we are away. I turn on the cartoons and line them all up on the couch before we go. "Be good," I say.

Mom and I are the first shoppers in the girls'

department. It only takes me a few minutes to spot a bathing suit I like, a shiny bright pink and white polka-dot two-piece. The top crisscross-ties in the front, making me look more . . . *more mature* than I am. I look at the price tag. It might be too expensive.

Mom doesn't make me try on the suit for her approval. She respects my privacy. "I'll wait here, go ahead," she says. When I come out of the dressing room smiling, she smiles, too. "Okay, good. Now go ahead and pick out a cover-up."

After I do, Mom helps me find a matching shade of pink flip-flops and then says, "Let's get you a hair band and some sunglasses." Our shopping cart is filling up nicely. When Mom sees my eyes rest on a tropical-island straw beach bag with pink and yellow trim, she says, "We'll need one of those, too."

"Are you sure?" I say, worried about how much this is all going to cost.

"Yes," Mom says. "You deserve it. Now, let's see where the beach towels are."

When the clerk rings up our purchases, I remind Mom that Dad told her to buy herself some new clothes, too.

"I know what he said," she replies. "And I know what I look like in the mirror. I've got my maternity bathing suit from last time. I'll wait and get myself some new things after the baby's born and I can get myself back on a diet."

That's the story of my mother's life. Baby. Diet. Baby. Diet.

"How about a cone?" Mom says as we come out of the store.

·"Sure!" I say.

We drive up to Wilson's and we order vanilla and chocolate soft-serve twists and sit at a picnic table to enjoy them. It is rare that my mother and I ever have time alone like this. I want to tell her about the pool party, but what if she says no? Letting me bike to the store behind my father's back is one thing, but the pool party might be too much.

"Isn't this nice, A?" Mom says. "Just you and me."

"Yeah, Mom." I look at her face. "I'm sorry I didn't stand up for you when Dad said those mean things in the kitchen yesterday."

"That's okay," Mom says. She smiles. "That was a pretty clever idea you had putting what you wanted on that sticker."

I smile, proud. "It's Dreamsleeves," I say.

"What?" Mom says.

"I call it Dreamsleeves. I was noticing how people put their wishes in that silver box at church where no one reads them and I thought maybe you could try wearing your dream on your sleeve where someone could actually see it and help make it come true."

Mom hands me a napkin. "You've got chocolate on your chin," she says.

Driving home, Mom says, "I like it."

"What?" I say.

"Your Dreamsleeves idea. It's catchy."

The little ones all want to see what I got shopping.

Callie holds my bathing suit up to her body. Dooley tries on my sunglasses.

"So it worked," Beck says, staring up at me, eyes wide.

"What worked?" Callie asks.

"She wanted a bathing suit, so she wrote her wish on a sticker and it came true."

"Really?" Callie says. "I want to try."

"Me, too," Dooley shouts.

"Me first," Beck says. "I'm the oldest."

"O . . . *kay*," Callie says, rolling her eyes, "but then me, I'm next."

Dooley stamps his foot. "No fair. Why am I always last?"

"You're not," says Callie, "Eddie is. Be patient, you'll get your turn."

"Where'd you get the sticker from, A?" Beck asks.

"Dad's desk," I say, "but just take one each."

Maizey calls. "Can you meet me in the park?"

Dad left right after Mom and I got home from shopping and so the coast is clear.

"Sure," Mom says, "go ahead."

Maizey is sitting on our bench by the fountain eating a Sky Bar. That's our favorite candy bar. I stare at her face for a minute . . . trying to see if she has changed . . . trying to see if we're still best friends.

Maize-n-A. We've been friends since kindergarten — right from the first day we met at the bus stop and sat in the first seat by the driver and held hands, feet not touching the floor, telling each other not to be scared, that school would be fun. And it was.

Maizey breaks off a square and hands it to me. I take a bite. *Mmm* . . . it's the one with the vanilla cream inside, my favorite.

"What have you been doing?" I say.

"Not much," she says, "but listen. I've got a plan for the pool party." She breaks off another square for me, it's the dark chocolate one, and she pops another square in her mouth, chewing quickly. "Tell your dad my family invited you to our camp up in North Creek for the weekend. Tell him my mom will pick you up Friday night."

"Your mom is going to lie for me?" I say, shocked.

"No . . . A," Maizey says, rolling her eyes, "of course not. She'll just think you're coming to stay at our house for the weekend. No big deal. You've stayed over before. You're my best friend."

That last bit makes me feel so good I almost cry. My best friend. *Best friend*. Take that, Snoop-Melon. "But what if my father . . ."

"But nothing," Maizey says. "Your dad's let you come for a sleepover before. Right?"

"Right." Two times in my whole life, both times for Maizey's birthday.

"And he doesn't belong to the country club, right?"

"Right."

"So how could he see you there?"

"True."

"And your parents don't know the Dandridges, so it's not like they're going to find out from them, right?"

"Right."

"Good. Another Nancy Drew mystery solved," Maizey says, clapping her hands together like she's closing one of those yellow-jacket books we buy at Woolworth's when we have money.

I laugh.

"And stop worrying," Maizey says. "All you need to think about now is getting some sun before the party. You're whiter than Eddie's diapers."

"His clean diapers, you mean."

We giggle. I tell Maizey about my new bathing suit.

"Sounds sexy," she says.

"Sexy?" I say. "No, just . . ."

"Well, in a glamorous Marilyn Monroe–Jackie Kennedy sort of way," Maizey clarifies. "But you need a tan and some makeup and why don't you squeeze some lemon juice in your hair when you're out in the sun to make it blonder?"

"Good idea," I say. I finger some strands of my long, straight, used-to-be-curly-blond hair that gets browner and straighter each year.

"Yeah," Maizey nods, opening another candy bar,

this one nearly melted. She licks the chocolate off of her fingers. She gives me half. "Sue-Ellen taught me about the lemon juice. She's got loads of beauty tips."

I eat the candy bar. I decide to be nice. "Thanks, Maize. Got to go. See ya!"

Later that afternoon, right after confession and on the way to the liquor store when my father's in his best mood of the week, I say all casual, "Oh, Dad, by the way, Maizey invited me to her camp July twenty-third for the weekend. Can I go?"

Dad's only half listening to me as he turns the dial searching for a song he likes. "Guess so," he says. "Unless something comes up in the meantime."

"Thanks, Dad!" I say. That was easy.

And I didn't even use Dreamsleeves!

When we get home, Mom is at the table typing, fingers fluttering like butterflies across the keys, clickety-clack, clickety-clack.

"I'm going to take a nap," my father says. "Wake me up in an hour, Mags."

I go to my room, then back to the kitchen, where I peek around the refrigerator to see my Mom's happy face writing.

What are you writing, Mom? Is it true or made-up? Am I in it? Are you almost finished? When you're done, can I read it? Can I please be the first?

So many things I want to ask her, but like always I hold back. The GANE is my Mom's dream and she has to decide when she's ready to put it on her sleeve and share it. For now I'm just content to see my mother's face.

Happy.

CHAPTER THIRTEEN
Perfect Timing

The human heart has hidden treasures,
In secret kept, in silence sealed.
— CHARLOTTE BRONTË

Mom sends me to Garbowski's grocery store, just about the same time she sent me that other morning. This gives me an idea.

I put on my favorite blue-pink-and-green tie-dye shirt and my fringed shorts. I wish I could buy a pair of the really short "hot pants" that are in this summer but my dad would never go for that. I give my hair an extra few brushes and squirt the fancy perfume my aunt Bitsy sent me for Christmas. It's much more sophisticated than the Love's Baby Soft I usually wear.

I wonder, did Aunt Bitsy have her baby? I wish Nana

would write. "Here you go, Frisky." I sprinkle in some breakfast, touch his rough shell. "See ya later!"

Checking my reflection in the mirror, I decide I need some lipstick.

In my parents' bedroom, I lift Mom's lipstick tube and makeup compact off the tray on her dresser. I notice her silver-trimmed hand mirror has dust on it, like she hasn't picked it up and looked at herself lately. Passing by Dad's office, I grab one of the labels from his desk. I quick jot *meet Mike* on it and stick it in my pocket.

Outside, I walk down the steps past Nana's drooping flowers (sorry, I'll water you today, promise) and sit on the bench outside her kitchen door. I open the compact, dab on some blush, and give myself pretty lips. Then I stick my dream on my sleeve and grab my bike from behind the garbage cans.

Checking my watch, *perfect timing*, I take the same route as before, and *kazaam shazam*, sure enough, just as I turn onto First Street, there he is, Mike Mancinello, biking toward me, looking all David Cassidy beautiful.

Quickly I rip the dream from my sleeve and crumple it in my shorts pocket. I stop pedaling, touch down my sneaker soles to the ground, and make believe I'm adjusting my rearview mirror.

"Hi, A," Mike says.

"Oh . . . hi, Mike," I say, looking up, eyebrows raised as if I'm surprised to see him. I adjust my mirror again.

"Where you going?" he says.

"To the store."

"Oh."

"Where are you going?" I say.

"Home."

"Oh." *Think of something to say, A.* Mike looks nervous, too.

"I didn't know you belong to St. Michael's," I say.

"We usually go to St. Joseph's," he says, "but we were too late for that Mass."

"Oh," I say, "St. Joseph's is nice."

"I guess so," he says. "Church is church, right?"

"I guess so," I say.

There's a long pause.

"Are you going to Sue-Ellen's pool party?" he blurts out.

"Yes!" My heart beats faster.

"Right on," he says, face lighting up happy.

"Are you going?" I say. *Please say yes, please say yes.*

"I think Sue-Ellen's sort of stuck-up," he says, "but if you're going, I'll go."

My heart is banging like the washing machine against the refrigerator in our kitchen when it's too chock-full of laundry. I'm surprised Mike can't hear it!

"Were those your parents you were with in church?" I say. "They look nice."

"Yeah, I'll keep them," Mike says. "My dad's okay, but my mom can be brutal."

"Really," I say, "how?"

"She knows I want to try out for JV football and there's a training camp my friends are all going to in August but my mom won't let me go. She says it costs too much, but I know she's really hoping I won't make the team. She read in the paper how some kid broke his neck playing football and she's afraid that will happen to me."

"Oh," I say. "She's protective, huh?"

"No," Mike says. "She's crazy. There's just no reasoning with my mother when she gets these wacky ideas in her head."

"Try this," I say. I tell him about Dreamsleeves.

He laughs. "That's wacky, too. But I like it. Can't hurt, right? Where do I get one of those labels?"

I tell him you can buy them at Woolworth's or Two Guys, but "you could just write your wish on a piece of paper and tape or pin it on."

He laughs, not at me, with me. "You're funny," he says. "But cute. I'll call you and let you know if it works. Can't hurt to try, right? What've I got to lose?"

"That's the spirit," I say. "Good luck."

I put my right foot on the pedal and push off.

"Hey, A," Mike shouts after me.

I turn around. "Yes?"

"Maybe we can hang out together at Sue-Ellen's pool party."

"Sure," I say, shrugging my shoulders all nonchalantly like it's no big deal.

"Right on," he says. "I'll call you." He pedals off like he's in a race.

Hooray! I'm so happy I could burst out singing right here in public, but as I bike away fear rises like the river after a heavy rain . . . *What was I thinking? No, no, no. You can't call me. What if my father answers? No!*

I turn to yell and tell Mike not to call, but he's already gone.

CHAPTER FOURTEEN
A Tropical Tan

Many's the long night I've dreamed of cheese —
toasted, mostly.
— ROBERT LOUIS STEVENSON

My dad is kneeling on the gold-green tweed couch in the living room looking out the window at the cars going by down below. He's not doing anything except looking at those cars, not talking, not drinking, just looking. Maybe even daydreaming? I move forward so I can see the side of his face. He always looks so peaceful when he's looking out that window at the cars going by.

I wish I had the courage to say "penny for your thoughts?" but I don't. I never do. My father and I don't talk about thoughts or dreams or anything important. The last time I remember us having a real heart-to-heart conversation was when he told me about another baby brother going to Limbo. That was six years ago.

Frisky is trying to climb out of his pool house again. "No, Frisky, you can't." I pick him up, hold him in my hand. His little scaly feet tickle. I set him down under his palm tree. Sprinkle in some food. "There you go, little guy."

Frisky's pool house sits on an old bar stool we brought up from the basement when we moved up here. It's right inside the door by our bunk beds. Once, the little ones were racing around playing tag — they really have no other place to run in the winter — and the stool got knocked over and Frisky scurried off. It took me hours to find him. Good thing I did, because turtles can't survive for long without water.

My parents are talking in the kitchen. I pause by the refrigerator to listen.

"Roe, please," Mom says. "Where's the new baby going to sleep? As it is we've got Beck and Dooley bunked up in a room with one tiny dresser. Eddie's in a crib in the dining room. He should be moving into a bed. Please make an offer on the house be —"

"I've got it under control, Maggie," my father says in an angry voice.

"How much more money do we need?" Mom says.

"That's none of your business," Dad says.

"What, Roe? It is too my business. I . . ."

"*I* run this family," my father says. "You barely make enough to buy groceries."

"But, Roe . . ."

"I've gotta go," Dad says, and leaves.

My mother uses the phone in my father's office. I hear her crying. I'm not sure who she's talking to. "Another mouth to feed . . . kids cramped in like animals . . . drinking all of our money down the drain." She sobs. "But even if we had the money, he'll never leave his mother. . . . She'll make him feel guilty, he'll never go. . . . Roe is all she's got left here now that Mark's gone. . . ." My mom sniffles. "All these years he kept promising we'd get our own house. . . . *We're never going to get that house.*"

I feel like a boxer punched me in the stomach. *Can this be true?*

My mother gets dressed for work. Her face is flushed red and there's sweat on her forehead. "Are you okay, Mom?" I say.

"I'm counting the days to our vacation," she says.

We go to my aunt Flo and uncle Tommy's camp the first week in August.

Me? I'm counting the days to Sue-Ellen's party. "Mom?"

"Yes?

"Dad said I could go to Maizey's camp the weekend of July twenty-third."

"He did?" She sounds surprised. "That's great, A. You deserve some fun."

A cicada drones outside the window. "It's going to be another hot one," Mom says. "Please get the hose out later and give the little ones a rain shower."

"Whadaya puttin' in there today?" Callie asks as I start making the grilled cheese sandwiches.

"I don't know yet," I say. "Got any ideas?"

"Chocolate," she says, and starts laughing. She offers me up a plastic yellow Easter egg full of M&M's. The Easter bunny (Mom) hides so many eggs every year somebody's always finding one in a closet or under a bed, sometimes two holidays later.

"It was under the couch," C says, and she and Beck double over giggling.

Cheese and chocolate, hmmm, I consider. "Hey, why not? You only live once."

"Can I pour the milk?" B asks.

"It's 'may I,' and yes, sir, you may. Just be sure you don't spill it."

"May I set the table?" C says.

"Yes, miss, you may," I say. "Thank you."

After everyone eats and goes down for their naps, I will put on my new bathing suit, slather up with Johnson's Baby Oil with a few drops of red iodine mixed in for color, and climb up the ladder to the black-tarred porch roof to start working on my tropical island tan. It's a gorgeous sunny day, not a cloud in the sky.

A tropical tan is such an important mission that I have sacrificed my one and only Beatles album cover to make a sun reflector. I slit along the top and bottom of the album, unfolding it out like an open magazine, and then I covered it with aluminum foil. When I hold it under my chin, the sun will reflect off the foil and tan me, probably just as good as any country club pool, although I have no experience in the matter.

The phone rings. I turn down the burner on the frying pan and go to answer it.

"Hello?" I say.

"Hi, A."

I freeze. It's Mike.

"Hello, Aislinn? It's me, Mike."

Speak, now.

"Mike Mancinello."

"I know, Mike. Hi."

"You said it was okay to call you, right?"

"Yes. That's fine. But just call me during the day."

"Sure, whatever," he says.

"What are you doing?" I say.

"Talking to you," he says, and laughs.

Beck is standing by the phone bench, staring at me. "Is it ready?" he says, meaning the sandwiches.

I swag my head back and forth and mouth "no," shooing him away with my hand.

"What are you doing?" Mike says.

"Talking to you," I say and we laugh. I look out the window at the cars going by.

"What else?" he says.

"Making lunch."

"Sounds good. I'm hungry. What are you having?"

"Grilled cheese."

"That's my favorite. I'll be right over."

A chill runs through me. "No!" I say in a sharp, loud

voice. *You can never come over. My father would kill me and you, too.*

"Whoa . . . just joking," Mike says. "Take it easy. I already ate."

I laugh.

Callie is pulling on my leg. "A, they're burning!"

Oh, no. "I've gotta go, Mike, sorry. Thanks for calling."

Out in the kitchen, there's smoke. When I take the lid off the frying pan, a cloud puffs up and there's an awful smell. I turn off the burner, flip the sandwiches with the spatula. The bread is sizzling, charcoal black. I try scraping off the crud with the sharp silver knife, but the sandwiches are ruined beyond repair.

Beck is at the table starting to pour our milk. He knocks over a glass. The glass rolls across the table and crashes on the floor. Scared by the sound, Beck lets the gallon slip from his hands and the milk rushes across the table and over the sides like Niagara Falls. *Oh, no, what a mess.*

"Dummy!" I scream. "What's the matter with you?"

Beck is stunned, eyes bugging wide like I'm an alien from outer space who just shot him with a laser gun. I wish I could take back my words, but it's too late.

Beck runs to his room and slams the door shut. I follow him.

"Beck, I'm sorry. Honey, I'm sorry." I try to gently peel his hands away from his ears as he lies facedown on his bunk, his whole body shuddering.

"Get away from me," he screams into his pillow. "I hate you, A. Go away."

I trudge back to the kitchen and mop up the white lake under the table. I squeeze the smelly mop out in the sink. I scrape the black coal off of the frying pan with a Brillo pad, rinse it out, and start all over again, slicing a slab of butter in the pan to melt.

Callie is sitting, elbows on table, fists clenched to her jaws, watching me. I know she wants to say she hates me, too, hurting her best friend Beck's feelings like that, but she's also hungry and so she keeps quiet.

This time I grill the sandwiches perfectly, dotting the little round chocolates on the cheese, popping on the top layers, turning once, twice, three times until they are nicely browned. I cut the sandwiches into triangles to teach Dooley that shape.

"Lunch, Beck," I call in my kindest voice, but he doesn't come.

Callie eats her sandwich without comment.

"Triangles for you today, D," I say.

Dooley doesn't look at me. He is punishing me, too.

When I sit to feed Eddie his bottle, he wraps his hand around my little finger. At least that's something. You can always count on babies to love you no matter what. Maybe that's why my father likes babies so much. They just love you anyway.

After I wash the dishes, I go to B's room, to try to make peace again, but he is sound asleep, his sweaty head leaning into his Lambie-Poo stuffed animal, his bat and baseball by his side. I wrap his sandwich in foil and leave it on a plate on his nightstand.

When all the little ones are asleep, I put on my new bathing suit, slather on the oil, and climb up and out on the roof. The sky is cornflower blue. A plane roars loudly over my head, leaving a wispy white tail behind it. The sun starts cooking me right away. The blond hair will have to wait. We don't have any lemons.

Later, I do a Dreamsleeves label and stick it on my shirt:

Beck, I'm sorry. Please forgive me.

When B sees it, he immediately reads his name. "What's the rest of it say?" he asks me. I point and sound out each word for him.

"All right," he says, "but three strikes and you're out."

I hug him. "Thanks, B. Come on, slugger. Let's go play some ball."

"Me, too," Callie says, "me, too."

CHAPTER FIFTEEN
Kitchen Camping

In the spring of '27, something bright and alien flashed across the sky. A young Minnesotan [Charles Lindbergh] who seemed to have had nothing to do with his generation did a heroic thing, and for a moment people set down their glasses in country clubs and speakeasies and thought of their old best dreams.

— F. Scott Fitzgerald

The next day I get up my courage and dial Sue-Ellen Dandridge's number, praying that she won't answer the phone.

"Dandridge residence," a grown-up woman answers.

Sue-Ellen's mother, good. "Hello. This is Aislinn O'Neill and I'm calling to say that I will be pleased to attend Sue-Ellen's birthday party."

"Let me get the list," Mrs. Dandridge says.

She's back on the line in a second. "Say your name again," she says.

I do.

"Spell it for me, please."

"Sure, I know. Aislinn is an unusual name."

"It's a nice name."

"Thank you, Mrs. Dandridge."

There's laughter. "Oh, no, sweetie. I'm not the missus. I'm just the maid."

The Dandridges have servants? Wow. They are richer than I thought they were. I wonder if the maid has to wear a gray uniform dress and a frilly white apron and cap like the ones on television. I start to get nervous about the pool party. What if my new suit isn't good enough? What if Sue-Melon can tell I bought it at Two Guys?

I can't do anything about the suit, but I can work on my tan. I'll need to make sure all the little ones are sound asleep first, though. One of them might try climbing up to follow me and fall off and get hurt.

Up in the shed, we say the pledge of allegiance, hands over hearts, proud faces turned to the small flag stuck out of a hubcap on the wall. B, C, and D look so solemn and patriotic lined up, chins in the air, "I pledge allegiance to the flag. . . ." Eddie is standing up in his playpen, hands clutching the top, thumbs sticking through the mesh netting, mumbling along in baby talk like he knows the words. I wish I had a camera to take their picture to send to my uncle Bobby and uncle Jimmy serving in Vietnam to let them know how much we appreciate their service.

The last time Mom got a letter from Uncle Jimmy he said his feet were getting moldy from tramping through wet rice fields and trenches, but he was sure better off than his best buddy, Wayne, who got his leg blown off in a land mine.

Please, God, bring my uncles home safely, and all the other soldiers, too.

I speed through school, teaching Beck and Callie the capitals of ten states, Dooley how to do upper and lower case G, and Eddie how to count on his fingers.

After lunch — peanut butter and marshmallow fluff because it's quicker than grilled cheese — I put on Mom's Chubby Checker album and I get the little ones dancing, dancing, dancing until I see Callie yawn. I read *Curious George Flies a Kite* in a whisper-voice and soon, good, they're all sleepy little monkeys.

Beck down. Callie down. D and E down. Done.

I'm putting on my bathing suit when I hear the key in the kitchen door lock. Oh, no! I rush to put my clothes back on.

My father is at the counter, pouring himself a drink.

A drink at one o'clock in the afternoon? This is not good.

"Where are the little ones?" he says.

"Taking a nap."

Dad chugs his drink down fast.

"Maybe you can wash and wax the floor, then," he says. "It's filthy."

"Sure," I say.

He uses the bathroom, the toilet flushing loud. Oh, no, don't wake them up.

He makes a call on the extension in his office. I hear him laughing loud. He's always laughing loud when he talks on that phone. I never know what the big joke is. Now he's really got a chuckle going. Eddie cries. Great, thanks for waking up the baby.

"Tell Mom I'll be home late," Dad says as he's leaving. "I've got a meeting."

I stick a pacifier in Eddie's mouth and rub his forehead and soon he's off again asleep, but all the commotion woke Dooley up. I try to soothe him down again, but then he sees Callie and Beck standing there and he wants to be a big boy, too.

"What are we going to do now, A?" Beck says.

"Something fun," Callie pleads.

"Yeah, something fun," Dooley repeats, giggling.

Think, A, think . . . I've got it. "How would you like to go camping?"

"Yeah!!" they shout, all excited.

I haul the big spread off of Mom and Dad's bed and lay it over the kitchen table, sides hanging down all around to make a tent. I get some blankets and the pillows from their beds. Beck's Lambie-Poo, Callie's Raggedy Ann, and Dooley's LoveyBear.

"All right, campers, in for the night."

They scoot in and snuggle under their covers.

"Now, listen," I say, peeking in the tent, using a very stern army-sergeant camp director voice. "All campers must take a nap. One hour. No exceptions."

Beck groans.

"And if you all take a nap without making so much as a peep, there will be a very special reward, a prize for each of you."

"A prize?" Callie says. "What?"

"It's a surprise," I say, then I smile and shake my head back and forth, eyes big like I'm picturing that surprise in my head, "and it's something *spectacular*."

Dooley claps his hands. "Yes!"

"But everybody has to stay in the tent. And if there's one peep. Even one. Nobody gets their prize."

They look at me and nod. Game on. The phone rings.

It's Mike.

"Your dream thing worked," he says. "My mom thought it was sweet, like I made her a valentine or something. I didn't tell her it was your idea."

"That's okay," I say. "It doesn't matter. I'm glad it worked."

We talk for a few more minutes and then I say I have to go. I poke my head into the tent and the campers all have their eyes closed.

Up on the roof, soaking in the sun, I feel pretty proud of myself. The little ones are safe and sound having an imaginary campout in the kitchen and I'm getting a tan for the party. I think about Mike calling me. How comfortable and fun it is talking with him on the phone. Maybe, just maybe, at the party, he'll hold my hand.

I start to hum "Leaving on a Jet Plane."

Ahh, this is the life, a nap on the beach. The roar of traffic on the road below almost sounds like ocean waves.

CHAPTER SIXTEEN
A Little Tummy-Ache

Beautiful dreamer, wake unto me,
Starlight and dewdrop are waiting for thee.
— STEPHEN COLLINS FOSTER

My first clue there is trouble comes as soon as I come down from the beach and quietly open the kitchen door so as not to awaken the campers and I hear Beck shout-whisper, "Hide them, C, quick.... *She's back!*"

Hide what, I wonder. I pull up a side of the tent.

Beck and Callie stare out at me looking guilty as convicts. Callie is chewing something *quick, quick, quickly, gulp, swallow.* Beck's got one hand behind his back.

"Give it to me, Beck," I say.

"What?" he asks.

"Now!" I shout.

Head hanging low, Beck hands me a plastic bottle —
the one that was filled with little pink baby aspirin just
last week. I remember the bottle was full when I saw
Mom give two to Dooley because his gums were hurting
from a new molar coming in.

I hold up the bottle. There are only three left.

My head starts pounding. *Oh, no.*

Beck and Callie are looking at me, scared.

"We're sorry," Callie says.

"It was my idea," Beck says.

Dooley's asleep. *Please, God, let him be alive.* "Did
you give him any?" I ask.

"No," Beck shakes his head.

"Are you sure?" I demand.

"Yes," Beck says, eyes filling with tears. He criss-
crosses his finger over his heart. "I swear, A. Scout's
honor."

"Me, too," Callie says, reaching over to grab Beck's
hand in hers.

"Did you eat all of them?" I say.

Mmm, hmm. Beck nods yes.

Oh my God. What should I do?

"I'm tired," Callie says, her eyelids drooping.

"Me, too," Beck says.

"We'll take a nap now, A," Callie says, laying her head down on her pillow.

"NO!" I shout, yanking her arm up. "You have to stay awake!"

They stare at me, small and scared.

From what I know from television shows, you're not supposed to let someone fall asleep if they've ingested something poisonous. You're supposed to make them throw up.

"Throw up!" I shout. "Throw up!"

B and C look at me, terrified.

"You've got to throw up, right now!"

"No," Callie cries. "I don't want to."

I quick stick my finger in Callie's mouth to try and make her vomit, but she bites me. "Stop it, A!"

"Leave her alone!" Beck says, punching my arm. He hugs Callie close to him. They are both crying now.

I run to the phone and dial Mom's work number.

The lady who answers sounds annoyed, but I say, "It's an emergency!" and she puts me on hold to get my mother.

"Stay calm, Aislinn," Mom says. "I'll call an ambulance and get someone to drive me home. Try to keep them awake. It will be all right."

Please let it be all right. Please let it be all right. Let it be. Let it be. Let it be. Oh my God, what if I've killed my brother and sister all for a stupid tan? Oh my God, when my father finds out, he is going to kill me!

"Beck," I shout. "Callie," I shout, loudly to keep them awake. I race to my room, pull off the bathing suit, and change into my clothes fast as Superman back into Clark Kent. I rub the oil off of my face and race back to the kitchen. "Let's play tap, tap, goose," I shout, yanking them up to standing position. "Come on, it's a new game. You'll like it." I gently slap Beck's cheek "tap" and then Callie's cheek "tap" and then Beck's cheek "tap." I keep slap-tapping them and shaking them and slap-tapping them, singing *"up, up with people"* as loudly as I can. Dooley's clapping his hands, believing the game. Eddie's starting to wake up.

Finally I hear a siren. I run to the window to check. The ambulance pulls up just as another car is turning off into our driveway. The man driving must be my mother's boss. Thank God Mom is home.

The ambulance people are kind to Beck and Callie as they lift them onto stretchers. Beck smiles at me and makes the little one-finger wiggle good-bye sign I taught him when he was a baby. That nearly cracks my heart in two.

"They'll need to get their stomachs pumped," Mom whispers to me. "Take care of Dool and Eddie."

"Dad said he'd be home late because he has a meeting."

"Good," she says. "That keeps him out of the way."

Sitting on the bench looking out the window, I cry as I watch them putting B and C in the ambulance. What a horrible, awful sister I am. My stomach clenches. I feel like I'm going to throw up.

"Are they okay?" Dooley asks, climbing up on the phone bench to look out the window with me, a race car in each fist. He's just now realizing this isn't a game.

"Yes, Dool," I put my arms around him. "They just have a little tummy-ache."

CHAPTER SEVENTEEN
Alone Again

If there were dreams to sell,
What would you buy?
Some cost a passing-bell;
Some a light sigh.
— THOMAS LOVELL BEDDOES

*M*y *father is going to kill me.*

Fear as bitter as cough syrup slide-burns down the back of my throat. Poor B and C are in the hospital getting their stomachs pumped. I can't imagine how awful that must feel. *Please, God, let them be okay.*

I stick Dooley and Eddie in front of the TV to watch a soap opera. I call Maizey. No answer. I take down the campsite and remake all the beds. I finish another load of laundry and hang the towels and sheets out on the line to dry. The flowers in Nana's garden are drooping. I haul out the green snake hose, turn the faucet on, and spray them. Oh, Nana, I wish you were here.

Back inside, I think about starting dinner, but I don't know how long they are going to be gone and Beck and Callie probably won't be able to eat anyway.

The phone rings. *Please be Maizey.*

"Hi, A." It's Mike. I gulp, my heart caught in my throat. He sounds so nice. I want to tell him what's happening here and so I do.

"I'm sure they'll be fine," he says. "Don't worry, A. My little brother had to get his stomach pumped one time when my mom thought he ate some holly berries. Pete kept swearing he didn't eat them but my mother, she's a nurse, doesn't take chances with stuff like that. It wasn't any big deal. I'm sure they'll be okay."

This makes me feel better. "Thanks, Mike."

"Can I do something to help? I'll come over if you want. . . ."

"No!" I shout.

"Whoa," Mike says. "What's wrong?"

"Nothing," I say. "I'm sorry. It's just my father's really strict about boys."

"Oh, you mean you can't have me over when your parents aren't home?"

"Yes," I say, not telling him the whole truth. *No, I mean you can't come over, ever, period. My father would kill me.* That's after he kills me for Beck and Callie eating the pills. I don't want Mike to know about my father. He might get scared and stop liking me. I'll have to find ways to sneak out and see him, keep him a secret. "I've got to go now, Mike."

I need to talk to Maizey. Sitting on the armrest of the telephone bench, perched in the window like a bird where I have a good view of the driveway so I can see when my father gets home, I dial Maizey's number again, starting to cry at the hope of hearing my best friend's voice.

Mrs. Hogan answers the phone. "No, sorry, Aislinn. She's out."

"Do you know where?" I ask.

There's a pause. "She went shopping," Mrs. Hogan says.

"With who?" I ask.

Mrs. Hogan hesitates. "Sue-Ellen," she says. I hear pity in her voice, like she doesn't want to hurt my feelings. "But I'm sure she'll be back soon, sweetie."

"Oh, okay. Just tell her I called and it's important."

Hanging up the receiver, the tears come like Niagara

Falls. Who else can I talk to? Nobody. Maizey's the only friend who knows about Dad. The only one who knows the truth. I wrap my arms around myself and stare out of the prison tower window, the old familiar feeling raining over me.

All alone again.

After a bit, the phone rings. Mom is calling from a pay phone at the hospital. "They're going to be fine," she says.

"Thank God," I say, and start to cry.

"It's okay, A," she says. "Accidents happen."

"But it's all my fault," I say.

"It's going to be all right," Mom says. "I've been telling your father we're putting too big a burden on you. Watching four little children all day long is way too much responsibility for a twelve-year-old. We need to hire a babysitter."

Mom's best friend, Ginny, drives Mom home from the hospital with Beck and Callie. B and C look shaken-up, but excited from all the attention, each holding three lollipops from Ginny in their fists. I hug them tight. "Welcome home."

Mom snuggles B and C together on the couch to watch TV, giving them each a Popsicle to soothe their throats, which are sore from the tubes slid down them to pump the pills out of their tummies.

I hug Beck again. "I love you, B."

"Love you, too, A," he says.

I hug Callie again, looping loose strands of her wispy thin blond hair behind her ear. "I love you, Cal."

"Love you, too, A," she says.

"We're sorry, A," Beck whispers. "You told us to stay in the tent."

"It's okay. It's not your fault. Just don't ever eat pills again. Do you hear me?"

"Yes," they say, nodding their heads as sincerely as if they just put their hands on a Bible and took the oath to testify in a courtroom.

Mom is in the kitchen filling a pan with water. "Macaroni and cheese, tonight," she says. "It's soft and will be light on their throats."

She looks up at the clock. "Did he say what time he'd be home?"

"No," I say. "Mom . . . I'm sorry." My voice cracks. "I'm so, *so sorry*. I don't know how they got that bottle."

"It's my fault," she says.

"What? How?"

"I didn't put the top on tight enough, and besides, we ought to have a real medicine cabinet."

"But . . ."

Mom swings around from the stove, comes up close to me. "Listen, Aislinn. You do as I say. I am going to explain what happened to your father. All he needs to know is that B and C snitched the bottle, thinking it was candy, and I called an ambulance. . . ."

"But you weren't home when it happened. I was in charge."

"Stop," Mom says firmly. "I will handle this my way, A. Do you hear me?"

"Yes, Mom. I hear you."

I go to my room and unlock my diary and pour it, pour it all in . . . all the worries, all the fears, all the tears, tears, tears, until I finally feel calmer, more hopeful.

Frisky is feeling pretty frisky today, standing on his back feet, tippy-toes. He looks like he could climb right over that wall today. I pick him up, hold him in my palm. "No,. Frisky. Bad turtle. You need to stay in your house." I place him on the bridge, roll a few marbles around the bottom for a little excitement, and off he goes swimming again.

There's a soft knock at the door, a little-hand knock. I quick hide my diary. "Yes?"

Beck pushes the door in, then restuffs the sock down lower where he can reach and pulls the door closed. He must not want Callie to hear.

Beck sits on my bed. He's holding one of the name labels and a pen.

"Don't be mad, A, but I wrecked two of them already. I tried to sound out the words and I got some but then they all wouldn't fit."

"I'm not mad at you, Beck. I'm proud you tried. Let me help." I put the label on my desk so we'll have a hard surface for writing. "Okay, now. What's your dream?"

"Go see a baseball game, just me and Dad."

I gulp and swallow. In that second it occurs to me that Beck and Dad never go anywhere together just the two of them. At least Dad takes me to Hoffman's and confession and the liquor store, but Beck just gets lumped in with "the little ones." Of course he wants some time to have Dad to himself.

"Okay. Let's start with 'go.' What's the first letter? Gu, gu . . ."

"*G*," Beck says, "that's easy. I know 'go' . . . *G* . . . *O*."

"That's right." I hand him the pen. "Print small so all the words will fit."

The door pushes in. It's Callie.

"Can you please wait a few minutes, Cal?" I say. "This is something I just need to do with Beck."

"O . . . *kay*," she says, "but hurry." She props the sock back and pulls the door shut.

"All right," I say. "Next word. 'See.' "

"*S!*" Beck shouts, "then double *E*, you taught me that, A."

"You're so smart. Are you sure you're not in second grade already?"

Beck laughs. "I'm sure, A. You're a good teacher."

CHAPTER EIGHTEEN
Jeffrey, Clarissa, and Flop

We are such stuff as dreams are made on;
and our little life is rounded with a sleep.

— SHAKESPEARE

After Beck leaves my room, his dream on his sleeve, I lay in bed thinking until Mom calls us for dinner. Thinking and worrying. What will happen when Dad comes home, when Mom tells him about B and C and the baby aspirin? Why didn't you call me back, Maizey? I'm sure your mom told you I called. Just when I need you the most. You're probably having too much fun with Snoop-Melon. You probably don't even care.

Every time a car horn beeps outside on the highway, I feel fear. Every time I think I hear tires in the driveway, I cringe.

When will he come home? How will he react?

Even if he believes Mom when she says it was her fault, will he still be mad and blame me and say I can't go to Maizey's "camp"? I'll never get to that party now.

My father doesn't come home for dinner. He's not there when the little ones get their baths and go to bed. Mom and I watch TV. "You should go to sleep now, A."

In bed I hug my doll Clarissa, my ears wide as Easter bonnets, listening for him to come home. It's embarrassing to admit since I'm almost thirteen that I still keep three toys on my bed. Jeffrey, the elf; Clarissa, in a red velvet dress and black patent-leather shoes, long white hair and blue eyes with dark lashes that flutter open and shut when I shake her head up and down, "yes"; and Flop, my one-eared bunny. My cousins', "the saints'," dog Brute chewed off the other one.

When I was little and Mom and Dad and I lived down in the basement and I didn't have any brothers or sisters or school friends yet, I used to have a bunch of stuffed animals and dolls that I pretended were my children. I took excellent care of them, telling them stories and singing them to sleep. I loved all of my children, but my favorite was Bo, a big brown furry teddy bear with a green bow around his neck.

After Beck was born and the "old Polish couple" moved out of the top floor and Nana said we could move up, my father gave me two black plastic garbage bags and told me to pack my stuff. I put my Tinkertoys, Lincoln Logs, Play-Doh jars, books, puzzles, and games in one bag. I put all of my children in the other.

After the big move up, the bag with all of my children was missing. I searched and searched, crying. *Where were they? In the basement? Maybe a robber stole them?*

Mom helped me look everywhere, but that bag was never found.

I cried and cried and cried and cried enough tears to make a river.

Two days later, Jeffrey, Clarissa, and Flop showed up on my bed. Where was Bo? Where were all of the others? I lined Jeffrey and Clarissa and Flop up in a row and questioned them every night for clues, but they just stared back at me, silent.

A few years later, I was nine or ten then, I heard my Mom and Dad fighting one night in the kitchen. I snuck out of bed and hid by the refrigerator to listen.

"Can't you do something about her wetting the bed?" my father yelled. He was talking about me.

"The doctor says she'll grow out of it," my mother said in a quiet voice.

"There must be pills or something. Her whole room stinks like pee."

"The doctor said some children wet the bed because they are afraid or . . ."

"I should have gotten rid of all those dolls," he said.

My heart started pounding. I leaned in closer to hear.

"What?" my mother said.

"Didn't you know that?" Dad said with a proud-of-himself chuckle. "I threw out all those smelly things when we moved. I knew we'd get her new ones for Christmas. But then she cried so much I dug three of them out of the garbage to keep her quiet."

I quick clapped my hands over my mouth so they wouldn't hear me scream.

He threw my children in the garbage? How could he?!

"How could you, Roe?" Mom was as shocked as me. "How could you be so cruel?"

That night I cried harder than ever in my life, enough tears to make an ocean.

After I discovered what my father did with my toy friends, with only three left, I decided to keep Jeffrey,

Clarissa, and Flop close as I could, lined up, one-two-three, right by my pillow, between my face and the wall, where I can keep them safe. And every night I rotate them, so that they all get even chances to be hugged.

I've forgotten the other dolls now, except for Bo. I decided Bo was found by a nice garbage truck worker on Christmas Eve who brought Bo home to his bedridden daughter who loves him very much and feeds him spoonfuls of honey. And Bo is happy.

Sometime during the night, I hear the fighting and jolt awake.

"What the hell's wrong with you?" my father is saying to my mother.

I hear the slam of the freezer, ice clinking in a glass.

"Leaving a bottle of pills lying around. What kind of mother are you?"

My mother is a wonderful mother.

My mother is lying for me. My heart is pounding. My mother never lies.

She mumbles something I can't hear.

"And where the hell was Aislinn?" he shouts.

Fear grips my stomach. *Will he come drag me out of*

bed? I want to hide, but I want to hear. If I can hear, I can handle things.

"She was putting laundry away," my mother says. "That girl works so hard."

"Well, she should have been paying attention!" he shouts.

"Roe," Mom says in the calm voice she uses when he's drunk-angry like this. "We need to hire a baby-sitter. A is just a child herself, and this is her summer vacation."

"She's *thirteen*," Dad shouts. "And who's going to pay for a sitter, Maggie, huh? What do you think we are, millionaires? You know my commissions are down!"

They're probably down because you're drinking so much.

"Aislinn's twelve," Mom says. "She should be out playing with kids her own age," my mother says. "She deserves —"

"Yeah," my father says. He slams his glass down on the counter. "We all deserve a lot of things."

Sue-Ellen's pool party with Mike now seems highly unlikely. Dad had said I could go to Maizey's camp unless "something" came up. This is definitely "something."

My father is yelling louder. I hear my mother let out a sob. Eddie is crying. God only knows how many drinks my dad's had. Do you know, God? You know everything, right? Then why don't you do something?

My fear turns to fury. This isn't right. My father can't hurt my family like this. We need help. Who can help us? Somebody has to make him stop drinking!

I used to think . . .

If only I sweep the floor better, he won't drink.

If only I fold the laundry better, he won't drink.

If only I keep the little ones quiet, he won't drink.

If only I get all A's on my report card, he won't drink.

If only, if only, if only.

Callie shuffles in the bunk above me. I hope she can't hear them.

It's Flop's turn to be loved favorite. I hug him to my cheek, kissing his brown furry face. "Good thing you only have one ear," I say.

I love you, A, he says.

"Love you, too, Flop. Good night."

CHAPTER NINETEEN
Mother Mary

I've dreamt in my life dreams
that have stayed with me ever after,
and changed my ideas.
— EMILY BRONTË

O n Sunday morning, I wake up wondering who I can tell about my dad's drinking. I also wake up wet. *Oh, no.*

I get out of bed, peel off my cold, clingy pajamas and put my bathrobe on.

The bathroom is empty. Thank goodness. There are pink spots from my father's vomit on the toilet seat. I wipe them away with toilet paper.

He throws up every morning now.

I run water in the tub and clean myself off. I wish we could get a shower like everyone else in the modern world. Dad keeps promising, but his promises mean nothing anymore. Maizey said Sue-Ellen has her very own bathroom with a shower and tub and a makeup vanity with a cushioned chair and a closet you can walk around in, clothes all hung in pretty rows with matching shoes underneath. That girl is so lucky. I bet her birthday party will be fit for a princess. *Please, God, let me still be able to go.*

Back in my room, I strip the fitted sheet from my mattress and stare at the little puddle of pee on top of the plastic garbage bag Mom makes me put down to protect my mattress in case of accidents like last night. How embarrassing. In the fall I'll be a teenager and I still wet the bed like a baby.

I put the wet sheet in the laundry basket in the pantry that's already overflowing with dirty clothes again even though I just did four loads of laundry on Friday. On second thought, I shove the wet sheet down into the bottom of the basket so my father won't notice. Not that he ever does laundry.

I turn on the teakettle and put a slice of rye bread in the toaster. When it pops up, I slather on some butter and Welch's grape jelly.

I take my breakfast to my favorite spot, the phone bench in the dining room.

My father is down below on the lawn. There are cans of paint by his side and he's kneeling on the grass with a brush in his hand touching up the statue of the Blessed Mother Mary. That was a gift he gave Nana for Mother's Day once.

Nana must be so busy helping Aunt Bitsy that she hasn't had time to write. I hope she's having some fun, too, riding the cable cars and going to the beach. I don't know any grandmothers who work like my nana does. When I was little I used to sit watching her iron her "work dresses," all starched perfectly, at her kitchen table for her job at Russell Sage College. She'd put on pearls and an overcoat with a matching hat and walk sprightly up the street to the bus, shoulders back, chin up.

I thought my Nana was a teacher. It was just recently I discovered she's a housekeeper. She cleans President Froman's house, starches his shirts, polishes his floors. She is also the vice president of the worker's union. The first woman ever.

The Blessed Mother sits about as tall as Callie in the center of the sloping lawn that is our yard, a hill too steep to play kickball on. It would be a perfect hill for sledding, except if you didn't stop at the hedges you'd go over the bank across the sidewalk and smack into the highway where you'd be hit by a car, *crash, you're dead*, and so forget about sledding.

Mother Mary sits all blue and white and silent, hands folded, fingertips pointed heavenward in prayer, surrounded by the rosebushes my father plants for her each year.

Dad stops painting for a moment. He bows his head, probably praying. He's getting balder on top, his dark hair ringed round like a monk's.

My father loves the Blessed Mother. My mom has a "strong devotion" to her as well. In May, which is Mary's special month, my mother makes all of us kneel to say the rosary in front of the small Mary statue we have on the buffet in the dining room. There is always a bouquet of fresh lilacs and a votive candle lit in Mary's honor. My mother makes us say that entire rosary, every bead, no matter what. No matter if the phone is ringing, or my father is yelling, or dinner is burning, we keep praying.

Sometimes I watch my mom's face as she prays, eyes closed, lips moving, often tears streaming down. *Why are you crying?* I want to ask, but I already know why. She's crying about the drinking. It has to be that.

I think of the Beatles song: "Mother Mary comes to me, speaking words of wisdom, let it be." *Send my dad some wisdom, Mary. Help him stop drinking, please.*

I walk down the back steps and across the lawn to where my father is working. He has finished repainting an area of blue on Mary's sleeve and now he's got his smaller brushes out, touching up her face. He doesn't notice me. I swat away a bee buzzing close to my face. A cicada drones nearby, heralding more hot weather.

My father closes one can, opens another. "Oh, A . . . What do you think?"

"Beautiful," I say. "She looks beautiful."

My father smiles. He looks like he's going to cry — the way he does when he comes out of confession. He nods his head up and down. "Yes," he says. "She does."

We all get dressed in our Sunday best and trudge up the hill to Mass. There's the old man in the brown suit and matching hat with the gull feather in the rim. Nana's friend Mrs. Casey asks if we've heard from her yet. She stares at Mom's belly. "Are you . . ." And Mom nods yes.

"Oh, thank God and his Blessed Mother," Mrs. Casey says, clasping her hands together.

Maria and Leo Carroll are talking with another young couple. Maria sees me, "Aislinn, hi!" waving for me to join them, but the organ is starting and we have to sit.

Beck's wearing his baseball dream on the sleeve of his shirt. Dad reads it and smiles. He gentle-punches Beck's arm. "Let me see what I can do, Buster Brown."

Beck's face nearly bursts with joy. It's like they're already sitting in the bleachers, eating peanuts and Cracker Jack. Oh, I hope it comes true for you, Beck!

After I receive Communion and return to our pew to kneel, I pray the same thing I do every Sunday. *Please, God, make my dad stop drinking.*

I look up at the statues. They stare back — rock hard marble, cold and silent. I look at the face of Jesus. *Open your eyes, please. I need you to see.*

After we walk home from Mass, my mother makes a big brunch, scrambled eggs and sausage, toast with jelly, cinnamon rolls, orange juice, and tea. We all sit, shoulder to shoulder, around the formica table with the Christmas-card propped leg.

My father looks excited about something. He gets a piece of paper, writes like he's making a list. "Got to get some things. I'll be back," he says.

When I finish drying the dishes, Mom says, "Why don't you go do something fun, A? Go ahead, get out of here."

I dial Maizey's number, no answer. No surprise.

I pack a lunch for later, bologna and cheese with mustard, a thermos of soda, some onion-garlic chips, and the Freihofer's cupcake I wrapped in a napkin and hid behind the breadbox yesterday. With so many people in the family, you have to take precautions. A box of Freihofer's chocolate chip cookies usually lasts two days; there are probably thirty in there, but cupcakes come six to a box, one for everyone. Once Eddie starts eating regular food, somebody's going to be sorry.

I put my lunch bag in my satchel with my diary and pen and sling my guitar on my back, then, checking that the coast is clear, I head up the path to my house.

Prisoner Number One, Aislinn aka "Dream" O'Neill, out on temporary parole.

In my Peely-Stick Shop I sing my heart out —

"Green-Eyed Lady" by Sugarloaf, "Cracklin' Rosie" by Neil Diamond, "Ain't No Mountain High Enough" by Diana Ross, and "Love Grows Where My Rosemary Goes" by Edison Lighthouse. I eat my sandwich, smiling at the happy words tacked on the trees: *DREAM. BELIEVE. LOVE.*

I think about how much I miss having Nana right downstairs from me. We are different, but we love each other strong. She keeps her feelings to herself, so proud and private. Me? I'd spill the contents of my heart to the milkman if he asked.

"We've got to toughen you up, Aislinn," Nana says. "You need to grow a thicker skin. You'll get crushed wearing your heart on your sleeve like you do."

I lie down, sun-stars twinkling through the pine bough roof, and take a nap. Later when I wake up, I walk to the edge of the hill, where I can see the river in the distance. There's a ship moving slowly by. Where are you going? I wonder.

I gather up my things and head back down the hill, where much to my surprise I see my father standing by the old outhouse. He's prying a board away with a long steel tool. There is a stack of lumber on the ground, and a window.

"What are you doing?" I say.

"I'm building Mom a little writer's house for her birthday," he says. He smiles, looking at me like I should pay him a compliment.

I would except, in that moment, I have all I can do to not burst into tears. If he's building her writer's house here, it must mean he's never going to build her one at our house in the country.

We are never going to get our house in the country.

CHAPTER TWENTY
Happy Birthday, Mom

But there's nothing half so sweet in life
As love's young dream.
— THOMAS MOORE

Dreamsleeves worked for Beck.

One of Dad's customers had a family conflict and couldn't use his box seats at the Yankees game. Dad took Beck, just the two of them.

When they got back from New York City late last night, I swear Beck looked like he was ten years old, not a "little one" anymore.

He taped the ticket stub and popcorn box and Yankees pennant on the wall by his bed, proof to him that dreams come true.

And we finally got a postcard from Nana!

"Greetings from San Francisco" with a picture of a cable car.

> *Dear Roe, Maggie, and Family,*
> *Bitsy had a boy. 8 lbs, 7 ounces. They*
> *named him Robert William III, after his*
> *father and grandfather. Baby and Mom are*
> *healthy. Love, Mother (Nana)*

I rush to tell everyone the good news.

"I want to make the baby a picture," Callie says, and I get out paper and pencils and crayons for the little ones. I write my aunt Bitsy a congratulations letter and send a letter to Nana, too.

Sue-Ellen's pool party is Saturday.

The good news is that I think I can still go to "Maizey's camp" for the weekend. I reminded Dad and he said he "didn't see why not."

The bad news is that Dad is drinking more, coming home earlier and earlier from work. If he doesn't make calls, he doesn't get commissions, and that means no house. I refuse to believe that dream won't come true. And if it's not the money, but *Nana* that's holding him back, I will talk to Nana when she gets home. I'll wear that dream on my sleeve. Nana is so proud of this house she raised her family in. My mother deserves to raise her family in her own house, too, and six kids need more than two bedrooms.

I wonder what Nana will think of the "little writer's house." Back when Nana and Papa were building their American Dream, clearing the land and constructing this house, before they got their plumbing installed, they used the outhouse for a toilet, like in "the old country." There's a quarter moon cut out near the top of the door to let the light in.

My father has been working hard to change the outhouse into a writer's house. He sawed out a square and installed a window. He stuffed rolls of pink insulation up and down and overhead, put up new walls and painted them, hired an electrician to install a light. He covered the old stink hole with a long piece of wood, then nailed wood around to make a desk, bought a new chair, and in what I thought was a very elegant touch, he hung a brass knocker engraved with an *M*, for Maggie, on the door.

Dad also hung a picture on the wall. It's a photo of Mom and Dad, the night of their senior prom. She's wearing a gown and a corsage. He's in a suit and tie with a boutonniere. They are wearing crowns, just named King and Queen of the Prom. Mom is showing off the diamond ring on her finger. They would be married six months later.

"What do you think?" Dad says to me on the morning of Mom's birthday, as he's polishing the brass knocker.

"It's nice," I say.

"Go get her typewriter and papers before she wakes up," Dad says, and I do.

I make Mom her favorite breakfast, two eggs over easy on rye toast with pineapple juice and coffee. B, C, and D give her the cards I helped them make in school. I give her the present I made up in my shop — a flower vase made out of a plastic laundry detergent bottle, with other chips of plastic glued on like a mosaic.

"Happy Birthday, Mom."

"You made this, A?" she says. "I love it."

I go to Nana's garden and pick Mom a bouquet, set the vase in the center of the kitchen table. "Beautiful," Mom says, "thank you, honey."

Dad comes into the kitchen all freshly washed up and in a blue shirt that makes his blue eyes look even bluer.

"Are you ready for your present, Your Majesty Maggie?" my dad says, holding up his arm for her to take.

"What's this?" Mom says, even though I know she knows Dad's finally ready to show her what he's been working on all this time. She's seen the purchases and heard the drilling and hammering.

"Oh, wait," Dad says. He whispers something to Callie and she runs off, coming back seconds later with the ballet princess crown she got for her birthday.

"Here, Dad, here," Callie says, so proud to be helping.

My father sticks the crown on my mother's head, pushing the ends into her thick brown hair so it stays. The little ones watch in awe.

"You look beautiful, Mommy," Callie says.

Dad escorts Mom down the steps and up the hill past our school shed, me behind him carrying E, followed by B, C, and D.

My mother smiles at the knocker. "Thank you, Roe," she says.

Dad opens the door for her. "Go ahead, Your Majesty. It's all yours."

There sits my mother's typewriter over the spot where the toilet used to be. I guess the GANE will be like my mother's garden, her story springing up from the old manure underneath. I sniff in. It still smells bad, but I would never say that. The window is open and there's a breeze coming in. Perhaps over time the fresh air will work. And there are the lilac bushes, too.

There's an envelope in the typewriter. "MY OWN MAGGIE MAGPIE," it says.

My mom opens it. A birthday card from my father. She reads the inscription, looks at him, and smiles with a look of total love. She sees the photograph he nailed on the wall, walks to it, peers in, her eyes filling with tears.

"I love you, Magpie," my father says, kissing her forehead, hugging her.

"I love you, too, Roe," she says, kissing him on the lips.

"Oooh, mushy," Beck says. Callie giggles.

"Come on, let's do something," Dad says. "It's a beautiful day."

"How about a drive to Crystal Lake," Mom says. "I'd love to go for a swim."

"Can we stop at Jack's for lunch, Dad?" Beck says.

"Ask your mother," Dad says. "It's her birthday. Whatever she says, goes."

When my family starts down the hill to the house, I stay behind for a minute. I stare at the photograph of my parents. They look so beautiful, so happy. That was the year they won three dance contests. Mom always says it was Dad who deserved the ribbons. "He just swept me off my feet," she says.

Their senior prom. Six months later they would have a fairy-tale wedding, a honeymoon in Niagara Falls. They would live in the basement of his parents' house, "just for a year or so" until Dad made enough money to get them "a place of their own." Dad would make a ton of money and drive a new Cadillac every year and buy my mother a house in the country with apple trees and a stream running by and she was going to go to college and write the Greatest American Novel Ever, and then they had me. *Sigh.*

Funny how they named me a name that means "dream," because I am very surely convinced that having me was the beginning of the end of their dreams.

One kid, two kids, three kids, four . . .

and every year my father drinking more.

CHAPTER TWENTY-ONE
"Out"

The eye of man hath not heard,
the ear of man hath not seen,
man's hand is not able to taste,
his tongue to conceive,
nor his heart to report,
what my dream was.
— SHAKESPEARE

Dear Diary,
Today my dad's drinking got worse.

This morning I heard the telltale clink of ice cubes in a glass in the kitchen before I even got out of bed. My father drank this *morning*, before he left for work.

So now my dad drinks all day long. Morning, noon, and night.

I mention this to Mom, but she just shakes her head and sighs, looking so beaten down. Things were happy for a while after her birthday but then the arguing started again. We haven't visited our house in the country. I'm afraid it says SOLD by now.

My mother has put on a lot of weight, even more than I remember with Dooley and Eddie. Her face is bloated and she's always sweating. Her ankles are as fat as thighs. Mom moves through the house like she's sleepwalking, like a zombie from that horror movie I once saw, her eyes sparkless, faraway, sadder than I've ever seen her.

She wakes up — goes to work — comes home — makes dinner — bathes the little ones — tucks them in — goes to bed, only to get up the same time the next morning to do it all over again. She doesn't go up to her writer's house. She isn't writing at all.

Dooley has graduated to real underwear now, no more training pants. He studies Beck's every move, determined to be a big boy, too.

After dinner Mom asks if I've seen Dooley. We search for him everywhere. "Dooley? Dooley?" The kitchen door opens. Dad walks in with Dooley in his arms.

"Don't you ever, ever try that again," Dad is yelling at D as he spanks him.

Dooley is screaming, "I'm sorry, Daddy. I'm sorry!"

"Please don't hit him, Roe," my mother pleads.

"He was racing those stupid little cars outside," my father says.

"But . . . I . . . I . . . I . . ." Dooley tries to talk between his sobs. "I thought . . . I . . . I . . . I saw my red one. . . ."

"He was almost down to the sidewalk!" my father yells at my mom.

"You could have gotten hit by a truck and killed," he screams at Dooley. He spanks him again and throws him on his bunk bed. "Stay there!" He shuts Dooley's door, pours a drink in the kitchen.

We all feel so bad for Dooley, but we don't dare go in there right now.

Later I see Callie sitting on D's bed, rubbing his back.

"I know how much you miss your car," she says. "Come on, I'll help you make a dream. It worked for Beck, remember? He got to go to the baseball game."

My father has another drink and another drink.

We all try to stay out of his way.

Nobody talks. Nobody says a word. Nobody wants to make him madder.

When I say good night to Dooley, I see a HELLO MY NAME IS label with a little red car drawn on it stuck on his pajama sleeve. As soon as I get some money, I'm going to buy Dooley a red car identical to the one he lost and say, "Hey! Look what I found down by the curb!"

My father's snoring on the living room couch, a full drink on the table.

I take the drink and dump it down the sink, put the empty glass back on the table.

The next day, my aunt Mary from Saratoga — who we usually only see at Christmas because my dad says all my "een" cousins are "noisy as a bunch of cats" and my aunt Mary "never shuts her mouth" — stops by unexpectedly with a quart of fresh, plump strawberries.

"Oh, thank you, Aunt Mary," I say. "Come on in."

Maybe I will talk to her, tell her how bad the drinking is getting. We aren't really close, hardly ever even talk to her, just at Christmas really, but she's family and . . .

"I have a doctor's appointment in Troy," Aunt Mary says. "I need to get glasses. Glasses. Can you believe it, Aislinn? At my age. I didn't think I'd need glasses until I was at least . . ."

Tell her, A, go ahead . . .

"Aunt Mary?"

"Yes, dear?"

Dooley walks out from his nap. "Well, look at you," Aunt Mary says, scooping him up for a hug. "You're growing like a weed. Oh my gosh, look at the time." She sets Dooley down, pats his head. "I'm going to be late, gotta run."

"Aunt Mary . . . can I talk to you sometime?"

"Sure thing, honey buns," Aunt Mary says. "Your mother's got my number. How is she doing anyway? She sounded so down the last time she called. You gotta take good care of her, A, with the new baby on the way and all. I tell your uncle Devon all the time how it's a crying shame Mags has to work. Raising five kids and another job, too."

Aunt Mary kisses my cheek. "Give your mom my love. Enjoy the strawberries! Hope to see you before Christmas!"

When the little ones are down for a nap, I make strawberry shortcake, my father's second-favorite dessert. His favorite is warm apple pie with a slice of cheddar cheese on top. I'm trying desperately to stay in my father's best graces, keeping the house spotless clean, getting all the laundry done, giving the little ones their baths after dinner — anything and everything I can think of to keep him from getting mad and taking back my permission to go to "Maizey's camp."

When my mother gets home from work, she says I can go out for a while. My father is at a sales meeting in Utica and won't be home till late.

I dial Maizey's number. "She and Sue-Ellen went to the park," Mrs. Hogan says.

"I'm going to the park," I tell my mother.

As I'm walking down the steps to my bike, I hear Mom yell, "Where do you think you're going, buster? Get back in here, Dooley."

I laugh. Dooley. That boy is fearless. Did he forget that spanking already?

Maizey and Sue-Ellen are on the swings — Maize-n-A's swings. They are wearing almost identical Mexican peasant blouses and hip-hugger jeans with embroidery around the bottom. I'm wondering where Maizey got the money for new clothes. She usually only gets new things at the holidays and her birthday, like me.

Maize and Snoop-Melon are talking and laughing, pumping their legs back and forth, trying to see who can go higher, just the way Maize and I always did.

My stomach flip-flops. I start to turn away.

"Hey, Aislinn," Sue-Ellen calls. "Come here!"

They stop pumping. Sue-Ellen drags her Keds sneaker along the ground to slow herself down and Maizey follows her lead. I walk toward them.

"Do you want to be in?" Sue-Ellen shouts in a voice that sounds like a challenge.

"In what?" I say.

"The club," she says.

"What club?"

"We're all turning into teenagers," Sue-Ellen explains, "me first, and when you're a teenager you're either *in* or *out*."

"In or out of what?" I demand, exasperated.

"Popularity, of course," Sue-Ellen says with a laugh. "My sister, Angela, who's in college now in Connecticut explained it to me. When you get to high school, everybody gets sorted out. You are either *in* or you're *out*. It's all decided by Halloween."

"We are going to be cheerleaders," Maizey says.

"For Halloween?" I ask, only half-joking.

"No, dummy, for real," Sue-Ellen says. "Cheerleaders are always in the coolest clique." She says this as if it's set in stone like a Commandment. "You need to make the team in eighth grade if you want a shot at the freshman squad."

"And how do you know all this?" I say.

Sue-Ellen laughs. "Well, *my mother* was the head cheerleader in high school. Her team went to the nationals senior year. My sister, Angela, was a head cheerleader, too. She taught me some great moves. I bet you girls haven't ever seen the . . ."

"Show A a cheer, Sue," Maizey interrupts, all excited.

Not needing a second request, "Sue" hip-sway-struts over to the grass. She rolls up the bottoms of her jeans, flicks back her hair, hands on her hips, starting position. And then she belts out a cheer, moving back and forth in perfect rhythm, shaking imaginary pom-poms in her hands. She ends with a dramatic soar, arms and legs stretched out into a great big jubilant X in the air.

"Isn't she great, A?" Maizey says, all goofy-faced like Snoop-Melon is her hero.

"Yeah," I say, "great."

"Sue-Ellen's been teaching me," Maize says, "so I'll be all set for auditions."

My stomach feels pom-pom pummeled. Maizey and I were going to be practicing together. But I probably wouldn't make the team anyway. Even if I did, I couldn't go to after-school practices. In September Mom goes back to working the night shift, four to eleven, and then the new baby's coming . . . who else will take care of the little ones? And besides, I couldn't go to the games anyway. The games are nights and weekends, and my father would never let me go . . . I was stupid to even think . . .

"I guess I could teach you, too," Sue-Ellen says to me, in a surprising display of kindness. But when her eyes take in my clothes and hair, I realize it is pity she's feeling.

"No, thanks," I say.

"My mother's judging," Sue-Ellen blurts out. "When the gym teacher heard what a great cheerleader my mother was, she asked if she would be on the panel."

"Good for you," I say, kicking a stone as I turn back to my bike.

"What's your problem?" Sue-Ellen says, hands on hips. "I was just trying to help."

"I don't need your help," I blurt out in a mean voice, wishing instantly that I could snatch those words right back.

Sue-Ellen looks like I slapped her, like nobody has ever talked to her that way before. Then a chilly smile spreads across her face.

"Don't come to my party, then," she says, shrugging her shoulders.

"I'm sorry," I say, feeling sick. I look at Maizey. She looks at the ground.

I can't stand this snotty girl, but this is my one chance to see Mike all summer. *Are you stupid, A? What's the matter with you? Get down on your knees, beg, plead.* "Really, Sue-Ellen," my voice cracks. "I'm sorry."

"Save your sorries," Sue-Ellen says, tossing back her beautiful hair. "You are out. Got it? *Out.*"

I look at Maizey. She stares at me, her face a jumble of emotions.

"Let's go, Maize," Sue-Ellen says, "we'll be late for the barbecue. Daddy's grilling steaks today."

I turn and bike home crying, Snoop-Melon's one word taunting over and over.

Out. Out. Out.

CHAPTER TWENTY-TWO
The Midnight Tea Party

We live, as we dream — alone.

— JOSEPH CONRAD

There's a crashing sound out in the kitchen and I bolt upright in bed.

"Cheap bill box," my father shouts.

He's talking about the brown wooden container hanging on a nail on the kitchen wall. There are three sections labeled in a swirly gold script, *Bills*, *Memos*, *Letters*, but the whole thing is filled with bills. It probably fell on the floor when my dad yanked it off to bring to the table, where my mom will be sitting with the checkbook and a pen and a worried look on her face.

Bill night is never a good night.

I open my radio-receiver ears as wide as they will go.

"What the hell?" my father shouts and I jump up,

fear burn-tingling like Fourth of July sparkler sparks all up and down my skin.

"Look what they charged for that ambulance, when you should've been watching your own kids."

I hear the freezer door open, ice cubes snap-crackle-popping up in their little blue-sectioned tray, then clinking down in a glass, my father unscrewing the cap of a liquor bottle, pouring it in, splashing in some ginger ale.

I wonder how many drinks he's had. I check the green glow time on my clock. It's ten o'clock. He's probably had six or seven by now.

"And I thought I told you to pay the electric," he says.

My mother mumbles something.

"Well, how much were groceries?" he says.

My mother mumbles something.

"What?!! What the hell are you buying?" he shouts. "I haven't had a decent meal this summer. All you feed us is crap."

That's not true. I get out of bed to go stand by the doorway near the refrigerator. *Mom makes good meals for us.*

"Food's expensive, Roe," my mother says. "And

diapers and baby food. A gallon of milk just went up again and a pound of hamburger is nearly two dollars."

Is that all? I think. *Two dollars?* I remember seeing a receipt for my father's booze in the bag from the liquor store. *Twenty-eight dollars and forty-four cents.* My mother could have purchased fourteen pounds of hamburger with that much money.

"You know my commissions are in the gutter," my father says.

And I suppose that has nothing to do with your drinking!

The refrigerator door opens, the light casting a goldish glow on the wall. The refrigerator is the only new appliance my family owns, everything else is hand-me-downs, or should I say hand-me-ups, from Nana. Mom wanted the "avocado" color, but my father said, "No, gold." I see from the hand that it's my mother opening the door, maybe getting some soda. I step back so as not to be seen.

"Well, maybe if you didn't eat so much," my father shouts, "you wide load."

I hear a shuffle and a yelping sound. I move quickly around the corner. My mom is in the refrigerator. She braces a hand against a silver rack to push herself back up. When she turns around, there's a line mark on her forehead from where it hit the metal.

I snap and rush toward my father. "Did you push her?" I scream.

My mother is crying. "No, honey, I tripped." Her hands are on her stomach.

"I'm going to bed," my father says. He swats the bill box off the table and kicks it across the floor, where it collides with the broom; the handle slams down on the linoleum.

I hug my mother. "He pushed you, didn't he?"

She shakes her head no, but I know she is lying.

"Just go back to bed, A, please," she begs me, wiping the tears from her face.

I hang the bill box back on the nail. I stand the broom up by its dustpan.

I hate him . . . I hate him . . . I hate him . . . I hate him beats like bongo drums in my brain. *What can I do? Who can I tell? How can I make him stop?*

I lie awake until I think of something to do.

Getting out of bed, the first sound I hear is the faint *tick, tick, tick* of the brown clock on the living room mantelpiece, the ledge that's supposed to look like a fireplace where we hang our stockings on Christmas Eve except there's no real fireplace and no chimney for Santa to slide down. I picture the chimneys on "our house" in the country. The house we'll never own.

My father is snoring on the couch. In the kitchen, I glance at the clock: nearly midnight. *Hurry, Cinderella, you don't have much time!*

I fill the teakettle and set it on a burner.

I take six Lipton's tea bags from the box and put them in the teapot.

I lift up the kettle before it whistles and make the strongest pot of tea I've ever made — dirt-dark brown like the liquor in his bottles.

One of the bottles is newly opened, not too much drunk out of it yet. I pour three-quarters of the liquor down the drain and then I replace the missing liquor with tea.

Maybe my father won't notice. Maybe it will still taste the same, but it won't make him so mean.

Back in bed I can finally go to sleep feeling better that I took some action. A little midnight tea party, we'll see if it works. At least I did something. I tried.

CHAPTER TWENTY-THREE
The Three Dares

The closer we get to giving our dream to the world,
the fiercer the struggle becomes to bring it forth.
— SARAH BAN BREATHNACH

In the morning I lie in bed listening to my father retching in the bathroom. It's worse than I've ever heard.

Good. Serves you right, for hurting Mom last night.

He vomits and vomits as if he can't stop. The sounds he makes are so horrible, I almost feel sorry for him, almost.

When he's finally out and I get up and go into the bathroom, I see what looks like blood in the usual pink and yellowy splats of vomit around the white toilet seat and on the gray and white linoleum floor. *Blood.* That can't be good.

At nine o'clock, summer school is in session. I don't have much enthusiasm for teaching or anything now that Sue-Ellen disinvited me to her party. I hate that girl. And, Maizey? How could she betray me like that? Not even trying to stand up for me?

Beck and Callie are working on their spelling lists.

"Today's the letter *M*," I tell Dooley, checking to make sure he's holding his pencil correctly. "Up the mountain, down the mountain, up the mountain, down the mountain." D is still wearing his little red car dream tag on his sleeve. It's got smudges all over it and the stickiness is wearing off, but he wears it every day without fail.

Eddie's gotten really good at stacking the donuts. "One . . . two . . . fee . . ."

I hear car tires crunching the gravel in our driveway. My father.

"Good job, class. Keep working. I'll be right back."

I walk into the kitchen. My father is pouring a drink. I stand there in the doorway watching him, frozen. Will he notice the difference from the tea?

He takes a swig, then rushes to the sink, leans over, and spits. "What the hell?" He picks up the bottle and sniffs. I try to turn quietly away before he sees me.

"What are you doing?" he says.

"Nothing." My heart is racing. "Just wondered if you needed something."

"Yeah," he says, "a better brand of booze . . . cheap crap." He opens the fridge and pulls out a can of beer, pops back the top, chugs it down, and then he's gone.

Maizey stops by while the little ones are napping.

"I thought maybe you forgot where I live," I say.

She squints her eyes like this hurts. She looks around my kitchen. I imagine she's comparing it to Snoop-Melon's kitchen. I bet hers is beautiful with all new avocado-colored matching appliances, maybe even a dishwasher.

I feel like saying, "Traitor, why didn't you stick up for me in the park? Why didn't you pick me over Snoop . . . ?"

"I fixed it!" Maize blurts out, all excited.

"Fixed what?" I say.

"You can come to Sue-Ellen's party again!"

Hope pops up like bread in the toaster. "Really? Are you sure?"

"Yep," Maizey says.

"How?" I say.

There's a long pause.

"Maiz — ey?"

"All right," she sighs. "I told Sue-Ellen about your father. About how strict he is to you and how you can't ever go anywhere . . ."

"What?! Maizey. Why? I can't believe you did that. I don't need that girl's pity. She already thinks she's better than me."

Maizey looks out the window at the bird feeder, a guilty expression on her face.

"Maize, what is it? Please tell me you didn't tell her anything else about my dad. Please tell me you didn't. . . ."

"Don't worry," Maizey says. "Sue-Ellen understands. She said she has an uncle who's a drunk. . . ."

"What??!! No, Maizey, *no*. You told her my father drinks? She'll tell every . . ."

"No, she won't," Maizey says. "I made her promise."

My blood is boiling mad. "You had no right to tell her my business, Maizey Hogan, and don't ever call my father a drunk."

"Well, he is, A," Maizey says. "Come on, you know that's true."

My heart is booming. "You need to go, now."

"Come meet us at the park at four thirty if you want," Maizey says.

Us? Uggh! *Us* meaning her and Snoop-Melon? *Us* used to mean Maize and me.

When she leaves I flop on my bed and cry. I watch Frisky trying valiantly to escape his pool house. He just gets to the top and then he slips back down again.

I am so mad at Maizey, but . . . I want to go to that party, to wear my new bathing suit and have fun like a normal girl and see Mike Mancinello.

I pull out my journal, the page opening to my "dreams for the summer." I knew the first two wouldn't be easy, but I still have a chance with the third. *Please, God, help me get to that party.*

When my mother gets home from work, I have chicken cutlets breaded and ready to fry, a lettuce and tomato salad, and potatoes peeled all set to boil. "Can I quick go to the park to meet Maizey for a while?"

"Sure," she says, with a yawn. "Just don't be long."

It's four thirty on the dot. They are not on the swings. Or the bench by the fountain.

"Psst. A! Come here."

Maizey motions to me from the side of the maintenance building. I walk over.

Sue-Ellen and Maizey are huddled behind a clump of tall bushes. They are both wearing hot pants and swirly-patterned blouses and big hoop earrings, another matching outfit. Is Sue-Ellen treating Maizey to all these new clothes?

"Wanna smoke?" Sue-Ellen says to me. Cigarette dangling from the side of her lips, she flicks the round top of a fancy silver lighter with her thumb, *click, click, click,* until a small flame appears. She sucks in, closes her eyes and smiles, and then blows the smoke out of her nose like a dragon, a beautiful blond-haired dragon.

"Here," she says to me, holding a red and white pack of cigarettes out toward me. Marlboros they are. I quick think how my mother smokes Salems.

"No, thanks," I say.

"Come on," Sue-Ellen says, "don't be a baby. All teenagers smoke."

"No, they don't," I say. I stare at Maizey like *come on, back me up*, but she looks away. Traitor.

"People who are *in* do," Snoot-Melon says.

"Guess what, A?" Maizey says. "They even have a 'smoking area' outside the gym at Catholic High. You can meet your friends there between classes for a smoke."

I consider this for a minute, this "smoking area" place. My father might control my life before and after school and on the weekends, too, but . . . you can meet your friends in the smoking area at high school — even friends who are *boys*? Interesting.

"Well?" Sue-Ellen says, smiles at me, not in a nice way, in a "dare you to" way.

"Sure, I'll try it," I say.

Maizey looks surprised, then worried all of a sudden. "But, A, what if your father smells smoke on your breath?"

"That's what gum is for, dummy," Sue-Ellen says, retrieving a green and silver pack of gum from the pocket of her shorts.

I notice a long, ugly scar on her leg.

"What are you staring at?" Sue-Ellen says, noticing me noticing the scar.

"Nothing," I say.

"A school bus backed over me and tore my leg open," she says. "Fifty-eight stitches, but loads of insurance money."

"Oh, I'm sorry," I say.

Sue-Ellen shrugs her shoulders. She takes another drag and blows out the smoke. "At least it wasn't my face."

I consider that for a moment. What a curious thing to say.

Sue-Ellen stamps out her cigarette. She tap-taps a new one out of her pack and lights it like she's an old pro. "Here," she says, passing the lit cigarette to me. "Suck it in through your mouth, hold it for a second, and then blow it out through your nose."

I put the filter side of the cigarette to my lips and suck in like I'm drinking soda through a straw. The smoke stings my throat and nostrils and I start to cough.

"Good," Sue-Ellen says, laughing. "One dare down, two to go."

I cough and cough and then I take another drag, this time just sucking in a tiny bit.

"What do you mean one dare down?" I ask, coughing, blowing the smoke out.

"You did the first of the three dares," Sue-Ellen says.

"What?" I say, confused.

"If you want to be in our 'in' group you have two more challenges."

"What are they?" I ask.

"Drink a can of beer and kiss a boy."

I stare at Sue-Ellen, wondering if she's going to say something about my father drinking. I repeat "Drink a can of beer?" as a sort of test to see what she'll say.

"That's right," she says, "drink a can of beer and kiss a boy."

Sue-Ellen and Maizey laugh like they know the punch line to a joke that I don't.

I take a stick of spearmint gum and chew it as I bike home. Three dares, huh? Kissing a boy might be fun, but drinking beer? No way.

All I care is that I'm going to the party again. Hoorah, hoorah, hoorah!

When I get home, B, C, and D can tell I'm in a cheerful mood.

"Give us airplane rides, A," Callie asks.

"Yeah, yeah!" Beck says, running over to join us, D following close behind.

"Me first," Dooley says.

"No, D," Callie tells him, "it was my idea."

"That's right," I say. "Come on, Cal." I push the dining room table and chairs back to make room. "Face me," I say to her.

I take my sister's little hands in mine and start to turn in a circle, faster and faster until her feet rise up from the floor and she's spinning round and round giggling and shouting, "Faster, faster!"

Beck is next, of course. "Do me faster, A," he commands.

I try my best, but B's heavier. I have to *turn, turn, turn* quicker to lift him up off of the floor, but then, finally, he's airborne.

"You're getting so big," I say, huffing from the effort.

"I know," he shouts, laughing. "Do you see me, Callie?"

"Yeah, I see you," she says, rolling her eyes.

And then, "Last but not least," I say, "Mr. Dooley."

D sets down his Matchbox cars and puts his warm, sticky palms in mine.

We twirl and he's off!

Dooley is light as a feather compared to Beck.

"Faster, A, faster!" he shouts as I spin him around and around.

His dream sticker falls off of his shirt.

Callie picks it up, sticks it back on him when he lands.

"There you go, D," she says. "It's still good."

CHAPTER TWENTY-FOUR
A Perfect Pink Tattoo

They who dream by day are cognizant of many things which escape those who dream only by night.
— EDGAR ALLAN POE

Do you smoke?" I ask Mike when he calls. I'm thinking ahead to high school, how he and I could meet every day in that smoking area between classes and maybe hold hands and then go to the cafeteria for lunch together. . . .

"No way!" Mike says. "I'm an athlete. Smoke kills your lungs, A, makes you not able to run as fast. Nothing's going to slow me down. I'm going out for football. Coaches don't let you smoke anyway. Besides, I think it's disgusting. I'd never kiss a girl who smoked; it'd be like kissing an ashtray, I bet."

Did he just say *kissing*?

"Why'd you ask me?" Mike says. "You don't smoke, do you?"

"Me?" I sound shocked. "No way."

"Good," he says.

"Why good?" I say, hoping he'll say what I want to hear.

There's silence. "Because . . . if I get the chance . . . I'm going to kiss you at Sue-Ellen's party. That's if you want me to."

Flutters flicker through me like I swallowed a seagull. "Sure," I say. "I do."

"Right on," he says and we hang up.

Later, locked in the bathroom, I try out various ways to wear my hair for the pool party. First, the pink hair band that Mom bought me at Two Guys. No. I part my hair down the middle and make two even ponytails. No. I part my hair on the side and comb my hair into one ponytail in the back. No. I try braids, no. A bun, no. A gold barrette clipped on each side by my temples, no. A head band with sparkly rhinestones. No, too fancy for a pool party.

In the end I decide to brush it down long and straight like Joan Baez or Julie on *The Mod Squad*. I did get some blond streaks up on the roof, even without the lemons.

Now, what about makeup? Can't wear mascara or eye shadow in the pool, no. Even I know that. But maybe lipstick would be fine. Especially if Mike is going to kiss me! I get a shiver just thinking about that. What will it be like to kiss a boy?

I apply some of Mom's pink lipstick, and then blot my lips with a tissue like I've watched her do. I guess that's so the lipstick doesn't smudge off on your teeth. Wouldn't that be embarrassing?

Good, my lips look good. I practice leaning forward toward the mirror, lowering my eyelids like they do on the soap operas on TV, but then I can't see if I look goofy or not, so I have to open them. I pretend my hand is Mike's face and I kiss it to see what that feels like. When I pull my hand away, there's a perfect pink tattoo kiss.

I smile at myself in the mirror. *You're going to do just fine, Aislinn O'Neill.*

I wash away the tattoo so my father won't see. I cannot wait until that party!

But what about the drinking beer dare? No way.

At night with a flashlight I write in my diary how excited I am about everything. How I can't wait to wear my new bathing suit and show off my tropical tan. How

I can't wait to spend three whole hours with MM, dare I say "my boyfriend."

> *I wonder where he will kiss me? Surely not*
> *in front of our class. Maybe there's a big*
> *beautiful giant willow tree on the country*
> *club grounds and he'll spot it and grab my*
> *hand and when no one's looking we'll run*
> *in through the long droopy green reeds*
> *which will fall back into place like curtains*
> *behind us making our own little secret*
> *garden. Oh, it will be so romantic. . . .*

There's a noise outside my room. I stop writing, ears perked on alert. I flick off my flashlight and listen, heart pounding. At any moment, my father could push the door open and catch me red-handed. If he ever read about MM, he would kill me.

There's a shadow underneath the door, like someone is standing there. I quick stash my diary under my pillow and make like I'm sound asleep.

I lie there for several minutes. When I'm certain the coast is clear, I turn my flashlight back on, pull my diary back out, and finish writing. When I'm done I lock it

back up and hide it good, lifting my mattress and pushing the flower-covered book way in underneath. Then I
stick the gold key down deep in Jeffrey's pocket.

I draw the little elf close to my cheek. "This is my
best summer ever," I whisper.

Mine, too, A, he answers.

CHAPTER TWENTY-FIVE
Stopping Traffic

The only credential the city [New York] asked
was the boldness to dream. For those who did, it
unlocked its gates and its treasures, not caring who
they were or where they came from.

— MOSS HART

The next day at three P.M., I'm perched butt on the phone-bench arm, feet on the seat, eyes peeled to the driveway in case my dad pulls in, when Mike calls me right on time.

"What kind of jewelry do you like better?" he says. "Silver or gold?"

Boom, boom, banga boom, my heart is drumming crazy as Ringo Starr. *He's going to buy me a ring? Isn't that a little fast? We haven't even kissed yet. What if I'm a really bad kisser?*

"I like them both, I guess," I say, "but I don't have much jewelry so either kind is fine." Beck and Callie are giggling loud in the living room. It sounds like *Lucy* is on TV. Gotta love that Lucy. Eddie's asleep. Dooley? Racing cars around the braided rug "raceway" in his room, no doubt.

"But if you had to pick one, silver or gold, which would you pick?" Mike says.

"Silver," I guess. "Why?"

"Just wondering," Mike says.

There has to be a reason. Maybe a locket or an ID bracelet with our initials on it? Ooh, how exciting!

There's a loud screech of brakes and horns honking on the road below. Something must have happened up by the bridge. I can't see from where I'm sitting. Cars are slowing and stopping. Mike and I talk on and on. He says he had tuna fish for lunch. I tell him I made grilled cheese with sliced olives. He said that sounds weird but he'd like to try it sometime. Mike says his family is going on vacation to Lake George in August, before football camp starts. I say how we always go to my uncle Tommy and aunt Flo's camp but how I can't stand my boy cousins, the devils. He talks about a movie coming out and maybe we can go together. I tell him how Beck did Dreamsleeves for a baseball game and it worked and how Dooley is still trying for that Matchbox car.

"I'll buy him one," Mike says. "Red, you said?"

"Oh, no," I say, "you don't have to do that."

"I want to," Mike says. "You could put it under his pillow and he'll think it's from Santa Claus or the tooth fairy."

"Dooley's still getting teeth, not losing them yet."

"Whatever," he says, and we laugh.

The traffic below has come to a complete standstill now. Horns are honking. I spot my father's red car coming down the narrow hill from Stowe Avenue.

"I've got to go now," I tell Mike quickly.

"Okay," he says. "Same time, same place tomorrow?"

"Yes!" I say, with a giggle. Hanging up the receiver I nearly pinch myself. Is this real? I have such a great boyfriend. How nice is it that he's going to buy a car for Dooley?

I stay perched in my phone-nest watching my father. He gets out of the car, walks to the street, and looks down the highway in the direction of the bridge.

The phone rings. It's Mike again. "I just wanted to know . . . are we going out?"

My heart beats faster. "I guess so."

"Good," he says. "Oh, and . . . do you like surprises?"

"Sure. I love surprises." We hang up.

Going out? We're going out! Wait till I tell Maizey!!

Down below, I see my father's hands fly up in the air and smack down on his head. Then he's off running toward the bridge.

"Stay here!" I tell Beck and Callie. I'm anxious to see what's happening. I pop my head in the boys' room to tell Dooley to stay put, but he's not playing on the rug.

"Dooley?" I check the bathroom, my parents' room, my room. "Dooley!" He's not in the kitchen, the pantry, or on the back porch. I'm getting angry now. "Come on, Dooley, this isn't funny. Where are you?" I check the closets, under the beds.

Oh, no . . . tell me you didn't . . .

I hear sirens outside. My body turns cold. *Oh, please, God, no.*

Please don't let Dooley be what's stopping traffic.

What if he got hit by a car? *Oh, please, God, no.*

CHAPTER TWENTY-SIX
The Worst Day of My Life

What happens to a dream deferred?
Does it dry up like a raisin in the sun? . . .
Or does it explode?
— LANGSTON HUGHES

I run to the living room, kneel up on Dad's spot on the couch, and peer down. A police car with a swirling red light and bullhorn *beep-beep-beep*ing is maneuvering its way through the blocked traffic. Beck and Callie inch up next to me to look.

"What happened?" C says.

"I don't know." I try to sound calm. "But stay here with Beck and watch Eddie. I'll be right back."

"Where's Dooley?" Beck says.

My body's an ice cube of fear. "And say a prayer," I yell as I go.

"Which one?" Callie shouts.

"Any one. All of them. Every one you know!"

I'm off across the porch, down the steps, past Nana's garden when I hear the sound of Dooley crying getting closer and closer. As I round the corner of the house I collide with my father, who is carrying my little brother in his arms. *Oh, thank God, he's alive!*

"Where the hell were you?" my father shouts at me, his face beet red, forehead dripping with sweat, jaw clenched.

Dooley's eyes are open. He isn't bleeding. He doesn't appear to be hurt. "D!"

"A!" He holds out his arms to me, crying, a blue Matchbox car in his fist. "The dream wasn't working so I went to find it myself and . . ."

"Hi, A."

I turn to look.

Mike Mancinello is coming up the walkway with a bouquet of flowers in his hands. *Surprise.* He is right here in my yard where he shouldn't be. Where he can never be till I'm seventeen. *Oh, no.* It's like the day turned to midnight. I feel faint.

"Who the hell are you?" my father shouts.

"I'm A's . . ."

"Classmate," I finish. "We go to school together."

My father's face is bloodred mad. "Well, she'll see you in September, then."

I turn to face Mike, his beautiful brown eyes look so confused, so worried for me.

"In the house, Aislinn," my father shouts.

"Are you all right?" Mike says quietly, sneaking a quick look toward my father.

"I'm fine," I say, holding back the tears.

"*Now*, Aislinn, you heard me," my father yells.

"Here." Mike hands me the flowers, looking confused and concerned. "Call me, okay?"

"Go," I say. "Just go, quickly."

Mike stands there. He wants to help. My body is shaking. "Please, Mike, *go*."

"All right, but call me," he says, and takes off down the side of the house.

Dooley is crying hysterically now. I turn back toward them.

"Here, baby, come here." I reach my arms out.

"I've got him," my father says, elbowing me with such force that I topple into the concrete drainage gutter, smashing down on my elbow.

My father hurries up the stairs with Dooley, pausing on the top step to look down.

Mike is walking back up toward me. "No!" I say, "please . . . *go*."

"Get up in the house and in your room," my father shouts to me. "*Now!*"

Elbow throbbing, legs soft as Play-Doh, I walk up to jail with my flowers.

This is going to be awful. The electric chair or worse.

Beck and Callie are standing in the kitchen clutching hands trying to be brave, holding back their tears. I see one of them gave Eddie a bottle. That was good.

I go to my room, stick the sock between the door and frame and close myself in. I look at Jeffrey, Clarissa, and Flop lined neatly in a row on my nicely made bed. I look at Frisky. He's gone! Oh, no. I look on the floor, under my dresser, underneath my bed. I catch sight of my face in the mirror. "It will be okay, it will be okay," I say over and over again.

It's only a matter of time until he comes.

When my father finishes spanking Dooley for leaving the house to find his little red car, I hear his shoes thundering across the hardwood floorboards of the dining room to my room. With no warning knock, the door swings open, slamming against my forehead. I fall back against my desk.

He lunges toward me.

"I'm sorry, Dad . . . I don't know how . . ."

The slap comes, open palmed and hard against my mouth.

My face stings like iodine poured on an open cut. I taste blood on my lip.

"Leave her alone!" Beck is screaming, standing in my doorway with his fists up like he's going to punch my father.

"Don't hurt A, Daddy," Callie says, sobbing. "I'll tell Mommy!"

"Go watch TV," my father shouts at them. "Now!"

He reaches for a clump of my hair and pulls me toward him, so close I can see the red lines on the whites of his blue, blue eyes, so close I can smell the liquor on his breath, from the bar he must have stopped at before he came home. "You're grounded for good, do you hear me? And stay the hell away from guineas."

He leaves. I push the door closed.

"I hate you!" I scream into my pillow, collapsing on my bed, sobbing. "Grounded for good?" I laugh like I'm insane. I'm already in prison, what could be worse? *I hate you! You're no father, you're a demon. You're not going to purgatory; you're going to hell!*

I'll run away, that's what I'll do. Hide out at Maizey's until the party's over and then hitch a ride to another city. No, you deserve worse than that. Maybe I'll sneak out of bed tonight and get that big sharp knife from the kitchen and plunge it in down deep till you're dead. I hate you for hitting me, for calling Mike a "guinea." You think you're so important being Irish, calling good people you don't even know awful names.

You're the one who's greasy and stupid and sneaky and evil. I'm going to tell everybody you're a drunk. I'm going to get you arrested. You're the one who belongs in jail. You. Not me. I didn't do anything wrong . . . and then I remember. *Frisky.*

Frisky, oh, no. I search every inch of my room. *No.* And I can't go look for him or my father might hit me again.

This is the worst day of my life.

It's dark and quiet. My mother is sitting next to me on my bed.

The fog of sleep lifts and it all rushes back over me,

the traffic stopping, Dooley, Mike, my father hitting me, Frisky gone . . .

Mom turns on my desk lamp and moves the cone toward me so she can have a good look at my face. She goes and gets a towel, soaks it in warm water, and dabs it gently against my lip. She cleans off the gash on my elbow. She goes and comes back with Bactine and a bandage. All the while tears are rolling down her cheeks and she's whispering, "I'm sorry, Aislinn. I'm so very, very sorry."

We hear the kitchen door open and slam. I jump.

"Don't worry," she says. "He's going out, not in."

Mom gets us a box of Kleenex. She brings me a ham and cheese sandwich and a glass of chocolate milk. She insists I eat something.

"Now tell me what happened," she says. "All of it. Every bit."

And so I tell her . . . about Sue-Ellen's pool party and Mike and how I thought I had gotten all of the little ones safely settled in before he called today, but somehow I didn't notice D sneaking out to go searching for his little red car. . . .

"This isn't right," my mother says, shaking her head. "There's no reason why you shouldn't be able to go to a pool party or talk to a boy on the phone. I told your father it was way too much to expect you to watch three children and a baby all day long. A baby would be hard enough. Watching one busy toddler would be . . ."

"You need to make him stop drinking!" I scream.

I take a deep breath. "Please, Mom, *please*. You've got to do something."

My mother's head drops till her chin touches her chest. Her shoulders heave up and she starts to sob, her whole body shaking with the force of a storm.

"I know, honey. I know. I just don't know what."

She says she'll get the little ones to search all over for Frisky. "Don't worry," she says. "We'll find him."

When Mom leaves, I lie awake picturing that sharp silver knife in the kitchen drawer.

CHAPTER TWENTY-SEVEN
A Brave Test

Do noble things,
not dream them,
all day long . . .
— CHARLES KINGSLEY

There's a quiet after the storm, like always.

Dad brings home onion-garlic potato chips and orange soda and three boxes of Friehofer's chocolate chip cookies. But I am way, way past food bribes for forgiveness.

I will never let him hurt me or anyone in my family ever again.

On Sunday morning I decide to test out my Dreamsleeves idea in a very brave way. I take a name label from my father's desk, snip off the HELLO MY NAME

IS — you'd think a grown man could handle "hello" without a reminder — and I print out a message with a red marker.

Now it's not a name tag; it's a dream tag. When we get to church I will wear it on my sleeve.

My plan is to be the first O'Neill to file into the pew, so there will be Beck, Callie, Dooley, and Mom with Eddie on her lap between me and my father, so that even if Dad does see my dream, he won't be able to do a thing about it.

What's he going to do, yell at me? I don't think so. My father would never raise his voice or cause a scene in church. He has too much respect or maybe fear of God and Father Reilly for that. Sunday is the one day Roe O'Neill is always on his best behavior.

My heart is racing, my palms are sweaty; it's almost time. After the Sign of Peace I take the label from my pocket and follow my mom and dad up the aisle toward the altar. Just before it's my turn to receive Communion, I stick my dream on my sleeve, right up top where Father Reilly cannot miss it:

Please make my dad stop drinking.

When Father Reilly extends the little round host

perched between his thumb and pointer finger and says "The body of Christ," I look him straight in the face, lock his eyes in mine, and I point to the dream on my sleeve.

The priest's bushy gray eyebrows rise up a bit. He reads the label and nods.

"Amen," I say, smiling.

He places the tiny white wafer on my tongue.

I make the sign of the cross and start back to my pew, nearly dancing I'm so relieved. Father Reilly will make Dad stop drinking. Mission accomplished. My dad will do anything that priest tells him to do. I don't know why I didn't think of this before! Well, I did, but confession isn't a place where you can talk.

The back-to-your-seat line is moving slowly. Maria Carroll is kneeling, hands folded at the end of a pew. She smiles a big sunshiny smile when she sees me. Then she leans toward me, staring at my sleeve.

Oh my gosh, I forgot. I quickly rip off the label, crumple it in my pocket. But Maria read it. I can see it in her face.

After Mass, when our family files out into the vestibule, Maria Carroll is waiting for me. She squeezes my arm gently, leans in, and whispers, "Come see me, A. I mean it. I want to talk to you."

"Okay," I say, "I will."

Father Reilly is talking to my parents. "I'd like to stop by for a visit later, if that's all right with you?"

"Yes, of course, Father," my mom says, delighted. It's not every day a priest comes to visit.

"Would three o'clock be okay?" the priest asks.

"Certainly, Father," my dad says, beaming with pride.

Alla-lu-ya!

Alla-lu-ya! Lu-ya! Lu-ya!

Thank you, God, thank you, God, thank you, God.

Thank you! Finally my dream's coming true!

We hurry down the hill home.

"A, please help the little ones change into play clothes," Mom says to me. "And then give them some cinnamon toast." She rushes to her room to change into a smock and scurries back into the kitchen before the toast pops up. "No time for a big brunch today," she says. "I need to bake a cake for Father."

My mother bustles happily about the kitchen, pulling out flour, sugar, baking pans, eggs and butter and chocolate. She even breaks a smile once or twice, as if a huge burden has been lifted from her shoulders. As if she, too, knows our problem is solved.

"I'm going to a car show in Albany," Dad says. Figures he'd leave when there's work to be done.

"Don't be too long, Roe," Mom says. "Father's coming at three."

I'm so excited I think I will burst. I mop the dining room floor with Murphy's Oil Soap and polish the table and buffet with Pledge. I set out a tablecloth and our holiday china dessert plates and cups and saucers. I fill the sugar bowl and the creamer, put out cloth napkins and forks and spoons.

After she finishes baking, Mom gives each of the little ones a bath and changes them back into their Sunday-best clothes. She's sweating hot from all the exertion.

"Mom, go get yourself ready. I'll take care of Eddie."

I dress E in a cute blue and white sailor suit and comb his wispy hair.

After the cake is cool enough to frost, my mother surveys the dining room table to make sure everything looks perfect. "We need a centerpiece," she says. She goes to the china closet and takes out the heavy crystal vase. It was a wedding present. Everything expensive we own was a wedding present. I love looking through Mom and Dad's white-with-gold-trim wedding album. They were so young and happy.

Mom hands me a scissors. "Clip some flowers from Nana's garden."

Outside, I snip daisies next to the gnomes. White-bearded Red is sitting on a tree stump, a book propped on his lap. The book is open and Red's staring intently at the pages. There is the imprint of a tulip on one page, a daisy on the other. One time I told Nana that Red "wasn't really reading" because there weren't any words on the pages. I was seven or so and proud of how smart I was. "He's studying how to make a good garden," Nana said. "That's hard work, too, you know." *I love you, Nana. I miss you.*

Bouquet in hand I turn to go in, but not before I admonish the brown-bearded, big-bellied, green-hatted gnome, Green, with the beer mug hoisted high in his hand.

"You really should stop drinking, Green. It isn't good for you."

CHAPTER TWENTY-EIGHT
A Holy Visitor

And even if this should not happen
merely to dream it is enough.
— PEDRO CALDERÓN DE LA BARCA

At three o'clock sharp, the front door buzzer rings. "Go let Father Reilly in, A," my mom calls. "And where is your dad?"

I walk down the inside carpeted stairwell to the first-floor landing, a staircase that hardly ever gets used and not at all now that Nana is away. I unlock the two locks.

"Hello, Father," I say, so grateful that he came I nearly hug him. This is it. The day I've prayed for. The day someone will make my dad stop drinking. My whole body is sizzling-shaking with excitement.

"Afternoon, Aislinn," he says, nodding his head with a smile and a wink. He smells like soap and Listerine.

He removes his hat and follows me up the stairs to our living room.

"May I take your coat, Father?" I ask. It hasn't rained in weeks, but better safe than sorry, I guess.

"Welcome to our home, Father," Mother gushes, first wiping off her hands on the apron she's wearing over her nicest maternity dress, then clasping the priest's hand warmly in hers. "We are so honored."

It's a really, really big deal when a priest comes to your house. The only other time I ever remember him coming was after we buried my uncle Mark and he stopped by the luncheon downstairs at Nana's.

My father walks in. Thank goodness. Imagine if I went to all that trouble and risked my dad seeing my Dreamsleeve in church and got Father Reilly here for a once-in-a-lifetime chance and my father didn't come home!

"Sorry I'm late," Dad says, all smiling, reaching out to shake Father Reilly's hand. "It's not every day we have a holy visitor."

My father is in a very good mood, all bubbly and cracking jokes. Hopefully that's because he had a good time at the car show and not because he stopped at a bar.

I start to get a sick feeling in my stomach. *Oh, no, what if Father Reilly reprimands my father for drinking right in front of all of us instead of in private? What if he threatens to hold back absolution for my father's sins and my father gets scared, or worse, angry, and takes it out on us when Father leaves? What if . . .*

"Let's have some refreshments," my mom says all cheerfully, like the mother on *The Brady Bunch*, motioning us toward the dining room.

"Here, Father, sit here," she says to the priest, offering him the chair at the head of the table where my dad usually sits.

"You sit here, Roe," Mom says, motioning my father to sit at the other head spot, which is where she usually sits.

My body is tingling, pins and needles all over.

B, C, and D are speechless. They just keep staring at the priest like "what the heck is he doing here?"

Mom offers Father Reilly a cup of tea. I offer the creamer and the sugar bowl.

Mom sets the chocolate cake trimmed with pink rosebuds in front of our guest and he nods most appreciatively.

"Well, look at that," Father Reilly says. He whispers

something to Callie and she giggles. "Yes, you can have two pieces," she says, giggling some more.

Dad smiles at Father Reilly like "isn't she adorable?"

Callie is loving all of this attention. We never have visitors. This is certainly a special day. Mom cuts the cake and I pass out the plates.

The cake looks scrumptious, but I'm too nervous to eat. *How will he do it? Will he ask my father to walk outside with him? Or come by the rectory later?*

Mom pours tea for my dad and me and then milk for the little ones.

Callie keeps trying to get Father Reilly's attention again. She leaves the table and when she comes back, she has one of the name labels and a pen with her. She motions for Father to bend down. She whispers something in his ear.

"Say that again," the priest says.

Callie whispers in his ear and hands him the name tag and pen.

"Well, all right," the priest says, laughing. "Let's give this a try." He writes something on the label and sticks it in the pocket of his black suit coat.

"No, you're supposed to wear it," Callie says, giggling.

"Let's eat," my mother interrupts. "Will you say grace, Father?"

"Certainly. Let us bow our heads and pray." Father Reilly thanks God for this "lovely cake" and for "this fine Catholic family seated around this table. Amen."

I open my eyes. Father Reilly is looking right at me. He winks and smiles like "don't worry, everything will be fine."

I sigh, relieved, the weight of the world lifted off my shoulders. I close my eyes, *thank you, God, for making my dream come true.* I open my eyes.

My dad's almost crying he's so proud of this happy family scene before him.

Mom asks Father Reilly about his summer plans.

He's heading up to Canada. He likes to canoe and fish.

I take a bite of cake and then another. "Mmm, this is delicious, Mom."

Beck says something funny and Father Reilly laughs and my father locks eyes with the priest as if to say, "I know, don't I have the cutest children?"

After a second cup of tea, Father Reilly stands. "I really must be leaving. I have a hospital visit to make."

"I'll walk you out, Father," my dad says.

Good. Now Father Reilly will be able to speak with Dad in private and tell him to stop drinking, or else. Picture that hot place worse than purgatory, buddy. *You know where.*

"Would you take an extra piece home with you, Father?" Mom says, extending a plate wrapped in foil.

"Oh, yes, Maggie. The cake was delicious. I'll enjoy this tonight after dinner."

"See!" Callie says, giggling, clapping her hands. "I told you it would work!"

"Yes you did, little one," Father says, patting her head. "Yes, indeed." He pulls the sticker out of his pocket. I lean in to read it. *A second piece of cake.*

I wink and smile at Callie.

"Here, now you try it," Father Reilly says, handing the dream tag to Callie. She takes it happily and sticks it on the sleeve of her dress.

"Now if I might just have my coat," Father says.

When I hand the priest his raincoat I try to lock eyes with him, but he is saying good-bye to the little ones. He makes the sign of the cross on their foreheads with his thumb, blessing them. My father watches all of this, face beaming.

I want to whisper "thank you" in Father Reilly's ear,

but I don't get the chance. No worries, I'll stop by the rectory tomorrow.

My dad turns the knob, opens the door, "After you, Father," and then they are off down the never-used staircase.

I go to my phone-bench perch in the dining room and watch them walk across the lawn and down the driveway to the priest's car. It's big and black and fancy.

They talk for a few minutes. My father's head droops down. He puts his palms on the hood of the priest's car and leans over. The priest touches my dad's back. Father Reilly gets in his car. My dad looks up at the window. I pull back quickly. Mission accomplished.

Mom is so pleased with how things went. I help her clear the dining room table. "I think I'll have a second piece of cake now, too," I say.

Then in a flash, my father rushes into the dining room. He picks up the heavy crystal vase and smashes it on the table, glass cracking, flowers flying, water spewing everywhere.

"What the hell were you thinking of?" he screams at me. "Embarrassing this family. Lying to that priest!"

I'm standing across the table from him, shocked and shaking. He moves toward me. I move away. He runs and lunges. I move faster. He's chasing me around the table. "Come here," he shouts, "come here!"

"No!" I scream, terrified.

"Stop it, Roe!" my mother shrieks. She's holding the kitchen broom high up in the air as if she might strike him with it. "Stop it this instant or I'll call the police."

My father freezes. He looks at my mother. "Yeah, right," he says.

"I will," my mom screams, her face crumbling with anger and fear and love and loathing. The broom is shaking in her hand. "I swear as God is my judge, Roe O'Neill, I will."

My body shudders as if I'll explode. B, C, and D are huddled in the corner crying. Baby E is yanking on his crib, screaming for someone to get him.

My father makes a sound like he's spitting. He grabs his blue jacket, the one with the muffler company name on it from when he won that trip to the Bahamas, and he storms out of the house, slamming the door behind him.

It's so quiet you could hear a flower grow. Something like peace settles over the room. My mother and I lock eyes. There's broken glass and water *drip-drip-drip*ping off the table, but neither of us is rushing for towels or a mop.

My mother opens her arms and I go to her. As she hugs me, I feel Dooley wrap his arms around my legs, hugging me so hard he'll cut off my circulation. "It's okay, A," he says. "It's okay. It's okay." Callie runs to hug me, too. Beck helps E out of his crib.

I tell my mother about the dream I wore in church. "I thought Father Reilly could fix things," I say, sobbing. "But all he did was say grace and eat our cake and get me in trouble with Dad."

"You're not in trouble, sweetheart," my mom says, stroking my hair. "No. Your father is the one who's in trouble."

CHAPTER TWENTY-NINE
Rainbows

The President last night had a dream. He was in a party
of plain people and as it became known who he was they
began to comment on his appearance. One of them said,
"He is a common-looking man." The President replied,
"Common-looking people are the best in the world: that
is the reason the Lord makes so many of them."
— JOHN HAY, DESCRIBING PRESIDENT LINCOLN

In the morning, I search everywhere again for Frisky,
not willing to give up hope.

"Maybe he walked to the river," Beck says.

"Yeah," says Callie, "turtles like rivers."

I feel awful. Frisky was my one and only and probably forever pet. My dad won't let us have a cat or a dog.
He says they stink and have fleas and bite.

My father is sitting at the kitchen table looking all sheepishly remorseful. He stares out at the bird feeder. He goes to the refrigerator. He pours a glass of milk for breakfast instead of his usual liquor. He doesn't look at me directly. He doesn't tell me he's sorry, but I can tell he is. He'll probably go to the store later to buy potato chips and cookies to try and make it better.

When the little ones run loudly through the house, he doesn't yell at anybody.

He goes to work and comes home on time for dinner.

Walking into the living room, I see my father kneeling on the couch in his usual spot, shoulders hunched over, staring down at the cars going by. I stand there watching him. He looks so lonely, so all alone. *What are you thinking? What are you feeling? Are you finally going to stop drinking? Why are you so strict with me? Why do you keep me imprisoned here? What are you afraid of? What? I love you, Dad, despite it all. I do. But tell me, Dad, do you love me?*

In this moment it occurs to me that my dad is in prison, too, the prison of dead dreams. He once was the King of the Prom, a handsome young man who won dance contests and drove a stunning red convertible, top down, fast, with no cares in the world, his whole bright life ahead of him. Now he's bloated from drinking and he's losing his hair. I don't think he's danced in years. His car is rusted and the next one will have to be a station wagon, not a Cadillac. There will never be ocean vacations or that house in the country with the stream and the apple trees. He's lucky he can feed and clothe his family. He is a hubcap collector.

Maybe Dad drinks to forget his dreams. Maybe they haunt him like nightmares.

Two more days go by and there are no more outbursts. Dad has one can of beer after dinner, that's all. Maybe Father Reilly got to him. Maybe my plan worked after all.

Maizey calls all excited about Sue-Ellen's party. When I put down the phone I say, "Dad, I can still go to Maizey's camp, right? Her mom said she'll come pick me up."

"Yeah, okay," he says. This gives him a chance to get back on my good side without saying he's sorry for what he did. "Unless something comes up."

"Thanks, Dad!" I go to my room, try on my bathing suit, practice kissing my hand again. A whole sunny afternoon with Mike Mancinello. I can't wait!

The third night, my father is drinking again, the hard

stuff, the brown liquor. He's out cold asleep on the couch at seven. And so it begins again.

How could I have been so stupid? The past few days were just the calm after the storm. My father erupts and there's thunder and lightning and hitting and crying and then *whoosh* the wind blows through and the sun appears and nobody mentions the hurricane. We're all just so grateful we survived the storm, we all imagine we see a rainbow.

No. No. Not anymore. I will not let this happen again!

"Can I go out for an hour?" I ask my mother.

"Sure, A," she says, sighing, tired, not even asking where I'm going. "Just be home before dark."

I bike straight to Maria Carroll's house.

"Oh, good, A, hi. Come on in," she says. "I've been waiting for you. I told Leo if you didn't come by tonight I was going to your house."

"It's better I came here," I say.

Maria nods. "I know. I know."

She pours us glasses of iced tea and sets out a plate of lemon drop cookies. My heart is pounding, my head hurts from worry. I want to tell her everything, all the bad things in my house, but what if Dad finds out? What if this only makes things worse?

"A," Maria says, leaning across the table to rest her hand on my arm. "I saw what you had written on that label in church. That was very brave of you. I am proud of you. Whatever you want to tell me will be held in the strictest confidence. Trust me, I understand these things. You have my solemn word."

Ahhhh . . . I let out a loud sigh of relief, feeling better already. Nana says a sigh is good for the heart. It's an Irish thing.

Then as if I just now learned to speak the language and finally have a way to communicate, I say everything, *everything* that has been happening to me . . . all the bad things going on at my house . . . all my fears . . . all my worries for myself and my mom and the little ones . . . Dad throwing up blood . . . it all gushes out like Niagara Falls.

Maria listens like she is a professionally trained listener, like she should be teaching college classes in how to listen. When I am finally done talking, Maria sighs. She smiles at me. She nods her head.

"Thank you, A," she says. "Thank you for sharing all of this with me."

Then Maria confides in me that her father is an alcoholic, too. And that she can relate to much of what I've told her. She says "alcoholism is a disease, a ravaging disease like cancer." And that my father "isn't behaving like this because he is a bad person or because he doesn't love you." It's that he has this disease and he needs help.

Leo comes into the kitchen. "Well, if it isn't our favorite teenager," he says, with a smile. Lee takes a cookie and chews it. "Mmm, good, babe," he says, kissing Maria on the cheek. "How's your summer going, A?" He takes another cookie and sits down. Maria touches his arm and tilts her head toward the doorway.

"Oh, I get it," he says with a laugh. "I know when three's a crowd. I'll leave you ladies to your gossip." He stands up. "Are we going to see your family at the Town Picnic, A?"

"Yes, we'll be there."

"Good thing. I want you on my team for tug-of-war, okay?"

Maria tells me about a group that helps people who can't stop drinking. It's called Alcoholics Anonymous. "If your mom or a family member or friend can encourage your dad to go to a meeting, that would be a good first step."

She slides something across the table. "I picked this brochure up for you."

"Thanks, Maria."

"And here's a list of places where they have AA meetings right here in Troy."

I look at the list, tears filling my eyes. Why do I feel like I'm betraying my dad?

"The hard thing for us to learn, A, is that no matter what we do or how much we love him, we cannot change the alcoholic. We cannot make him stop drinking."

A sob escapes, my throat clenches.

We cannot make him stop drinking.

"I tried so hard," I sob.

Maria hugs me. She hands me a box of tissues. She strokes my hair. "I know, sweet girl, I know. We cannot control the person who's drinking. All we can control is our reaction to his or her behavior. I know this may be hard for you to understand, A. It takes time. We have to protect ourselves and take care of ourselves. That's where this other group called Al-Anon comes in. It helps support the family of an alcoholic."

She gives me another brochure and a sheet with

meeting times. "I go to this one," she says, pointing. "I'd love to take you and your mother with me next week."

When I get home, I tell Mom to come to my room. "It's important."

I give her the brochures and tell her what Maria told me.

"Thank you, A," she says. "Maria is a good neighbor, a good friend. This is very helpful." Her eyes fill up with tears. "Let me think about this. Let me see what I can do."

The phone rings. Mom stuffs the brochures in her smock pocket and turns to go answer it. I follow her out of my room.

My father has reached the phone first.

"Hello?" he says, looking out the dining room window. "Who's this?" he says loudly.

The tone of Dad's voice makes me freeze.

"Mike? Mike who?" my father says angrily.

Oh, no.

"She's not here," Dad says, slamming down the receiver.

He turns around. "Who's this boy calling you?"

"Nobody," I say, my heart pounding. "Just a friend from school."

"That long-haired guinea who showed up the day you nearly killed Dooley?"

"No, Dad," I say, getting angry again.

"You know the rules. No boys. No boys till you graduate."

"I know, Dad. I know." *Please, God, don't let him say I can't go to Maizey's.*

My father gets a drink. He comes back. "And don't forget you're grounded."

"But, Dad" — I try to be calm — "you said I could go to Maizey's camp, remember?"

"Forget it," my father says.

"But, Dad," I plead.

"Go to your room," he shouts.

"Dad, *please*." I look to my mother for help, but like always she keeps silent, trying not to make him angrier, trying to "keep the peace."

Just for once, Mom, just for once. Couldn't you take my side?

I force myself not to cry, try to sound respectful. "Dad, *please*, you said I could. . . ."

"That's before you almost let your little brother get killed and shamed this family with Father Reilly and started sneaking around with boys."

"I'm not sneaking around!"

"Shut up!" he says, case closed, judge's gavel pounding down.

The prison door slides shut, *clank*, and the iron bolt locks into place.

CHAPTER THIRTY
A Miracle

Dreams are necessary to life.
— Anaïs Nin

It's the day of Sue-Ellen's pool party. Sunlight is streaming in the window. It will be a beautiful, blue sky, picture-perfect summer day. *Uggh* . . .

I roll over and stare miserably at Clarissa, Jeffrey, and Flop. They stare back at me silently. The drone of a motor revs up outside. My father is mowing the lawn.

I think about my new pink bathing suit and cover-up and flip-flops and straw bag. I think about how Mike and I were going to hold hands or even kiss, under that swooping willow tree that I am certain is at that country club.

Mike already knows my father is a tyrant; when he finds out I can't even go to a pool party, he will probably break up with me. Who wants a girlfriend who can't ever go anywhere? Who wants a best friend who can't ever go anywhere? I've probably lost Maizey to Sue-Ellen for good.

I lie here hopeless and dejected, overwhelmed with the injustice of all of this. I say a prayer and then another, but what's called for here is a miracle.

Then I hear "Dreamsleeves" in my head.

Dreamsleeves. Dreamsleeves.

Is that you, God, answering me?

I rip a piece of paper from a notebook on my desk. I write:

The Pool Party, Please!

I find a safety pin and attach my dream to my sleeve.

This dreamer needs a dream-helper.

Maybe sometimes the one person who can make your particular dream come true is a stranger you pass on the street, or a nice lady you know from church who just needed a clue, or maybe sometimes, that person is standing in your own kitchen.

I take a deep breath and go.

My mother is at the stove sticking a fork into one of the peeled white potatoes bobbing around in the tall silver pot. Potato salad for dinner later, probably.

I walk over to her, touch her arm, and lock my eyes with hers. I point to my dream and she reads it. She pierces another potato.

"These need a few more minutes," she says, setting the fork down.

"Mom, please," I say. "I'm begging you. I have to go to this party. I've been looking forward to it all summer. All my friends are going. Please."

The lawn mower drones closer as my father reaches the border of the lawn by the kitchen window and then grows fainter as he turns and heads in the other direction. The freshly mowed grass smells hopeful.

Steam is rising up on my mother's face. She closes her eyes and sighs and for a moment she looks younger, like a fancy lady enjoying a sauna at a country club. The slightest bit of a smile moves across her lips as if she's imagining something pleasant. The bubbling water rises to the rim of the pot and some water splashes over and down the side, making a sizzling sound when it hits the burner.

Mom opens her eyes and looks at me.

It's as if she sees me for the very first time.

"You are going to that party," she says. "If it kills me, you are going."

"Oh, Mom, thank you!" I hug her, giddy with excitement.

Mom turns the burner off. She looks out the window, then up at the clock. "I'll make him a big roast beef sandwich when he comes in," she says. "There's a show on he'll want to watch. Get ready and wait in your room and when I tell you the coast is clear, run to Maizey's and grab a ride to the party. But you've got to come right home afterward."

"Oh, Mom, thank you, *thank you*." I hug her.

I phone Maizey and tell her the good news.

"What did you get her?" Maizey says.

"Huh?" I ask.

"Sue-Ellen, for her birthday. What did you buy her?"

Oh, no. "I don't have anything. I didn't think I was going to be able to go."

"No sweat," Maizey says. "I'll sign your name on my card, too."

"Thanks, Maize."

"What are best friends for?" she says.

I'm waiting all dressed in my room. Callie is playing with Raggedy Ann up on her bunk. She leans over. "You look like a movie star," she says.

"Thanks, C. But don't say anything to Dad."

She taps her finger to her lips. "Just our secret," she says.

My mother knocks softly and enters, stuffing in the sock and pulling the door closed behind her. She is carrying two pillows.

"You look pretty," she whispers, tucking a strand of hair behind my ear. She turns back the cover on my bed and lays the pillows down, puffing them into the shape of a person, a girl who isn't feeling well and whose mother said to rest.

"What he doesn't know won't hurt him," Mom says. She looks up at Callie.

Callie taps her finger to her lips. Mom taps her finger to hers. I tap my finger to mine. Just us girls.

My mother opens up the door and peeks out toward the living room where I can hear an uproar of clapping on TV and a sports announcer shouting.

"Did you see that, Dad?" Beck says. But my father is snoring, out cold.

"Mission accomplished," Mom says, turning back toward me.

She takes my face in her hands. "I love you, sweetheart. Have fun. And don't worry. I've got this under control."

I hug her quickly and then I'm off, rushing out across the porch, down the back stairs, past the gnomes, across the lawn and the crunch-gravelly driveway. When I reach the sidewalk, I run.

Red Alert! Red Alert! All Points Bulletin, APB, Convict Number One, Aislinn aka "Dream" O'Neill, has escaped from Maximum Security. Turn on the searchlights. Set loose the guard dogs. A million-dollar reward has been posted for information leading to the capture of this dangerous fugitive from justice last spotted heading to her best friend's house in a pink cover-up with matching flip-flops. She has a tropical tan, and highlights in her hair. She is disguised with sunglasses and armed with a straw beach bag. . . .

Ha-ha! I'm laughing and running, bubbling over happy.

Free, free, free.

CHAPTER THIRTY-ONE
Our Own Secret Garden

There was a time when meadow, grove, and stream,
The earth, and every common sight,
To me did seem
Appareled in celestial light,
The glory and the freshness of a dream.
— WILLIAM WORDSWORTH

Mr. Hogan drives me and Maizey to the party. At the two cobblestone pillars with lanterns on top and the sign for Valleyview Country Club, Mr. Hogan turns the station wagon off the main street and we head up a long and windy road, bordered by trees — no willow trees, though — finally ending in front of matching stone buildings with navy-blue awnings, a large fountain with cherubs in the center outside.

So this is a country club.

As we get out of the car, two men drive by in a little white cart. One tips his checkered cap and nods to us. I look out over the golf course, acres and acres of lush green grass, dotted here and there with little flags. *Whaaaaack* . . . there's the sound of a club against a ball as a golfer tees off. Two other golfers cup their hands over their eyes to block the sun and afford a better view of where the ball lands.

"Hi, Maize. Hi, Aislinn," Sue-Ellen says, walking toward us, looking gorgeous. "You're the first ones here. Welcome."

"Thank you for inviting me," I say.

"You look nice, Aislinn," Sue-Ellen says, throwing me a doggy-bone.

"Thanks," I say. "You, too."

Sue-Ellen glows in the compliment, laughing in agreement. "It feels so good to be thirteen," she says. "Just wait until you two see."

The birthday girl takes our hands and pulls us into the Ladies Lounge. She checks to make sure "the coast is clear."

I look at my reflection in the long mirror and smile. I can't wait to see Mike.

"Today's the day you do the other two dares," Sue-Ellen says.

Kissing a boy and drinking a can of beer, I remember from the park.

"I already did them, last week at my parents' garden party, now today's your turn." She points to me and Maizey.

"Kissing a boy and drinking a can of beer," Maizey says.

"There are lots of cute boys to choose from," Sue-Ellen says. "Except keep away from Eddie Downes. I decided this morning that I'm going out with him next. He'll be captain of the football team and I'll be head cheerleader. Match made in heaven, huh? You can have Billy Hopewell now, Maizey, if you still like him. He was a decent boyfriend and he's a good kisser."

Maizey likes Billy Hopewell? Where I have been? And I can't believe Snoop-Melon's bequeathing boyfriends like a queen tossing pennies to the paupers. How would Eddie and Billy feel if they heard her talking about them like that?

"Wait until you meet my cousin Abbey from

Philadelphia," Sue-Ellen says. "She's fifteen and soooo sophisticated. She promised she would put some beer cans into a little blue cooler over behind the country-club coolers where our sodas are. All you need to do is sneak a beer into your beach bag and drink it out in the woods or somewhere. Just don't let my parents see, of course."

"Of course," Maizey says.

I look at Maizey like "are you kidding me? You're going to drink beer?"

"I need a touch-up," Sue-Ellen says, ruffling through her makeup bag.

Maizey turns so Sue-Ellen can't see. She winks at me and ever so imperceptibly shakes her head and mouths the words, "No way; I'm not drinking beer."

I smile, liking our little secret.

"But you've got to show me the empty beer can for proof," Sue-Ellen says, snapping her makeup bag shut.

She needs proof?

Maizey grabs my hand and squeezes it. I purse my lips so as not to giggle.

"I'll take your word for it, though, if you say you kissed a boy," Sue-Ellen says. "I can always check by asking him, right?" She throws her head back laughing. She looks at her watch. "I'm so excited. I need a smoke." She fishes in her beach bag and pulls out a pack of cigarettes.

The ladies' room door swings open and an attractive older woman in a monogrammed yellow sweater and pink plaid shorts enters. Sue-Ellen stuffs the cigarettes back in her bag. "Oh, hello, Aunt Delores," she says. "Let me introduce you to my friends."

Mike is late getting to the party. We've all already been swimming and Mrs. Dandridge just announced "luncheon is served."

I watch as Mike stands there looking uncomfortable holding a towel and a small box with a bow on it. Sue-Ellen's present. He scans the faces around the pool. When he sees mine, he smiles. I wave and he walks toward me.

My heart's a birthday balloon ready to pop.

"And so we meet again," he says in a sweet old-fashioned way.

I wish my mom could meet Mike. I know she would approve.

"It's been so long," he says. "I almost forgot what you looked like."

"Oh," I say, nervous, remembering the ugly scene in the yard with my father.

"So pretty," he says.

"What?" I say.

"You. You're so pretty. Are you sure I'm good enough for you?"

"I'm sure," I say, and we laugh.

Mike puts the present on the gift table. "What did you get her?" I ask, faintly jealous.

"My mom got her earrings," he said. "Thanks for telling me silver."

Oh . . . so that's why he asked about silver or gold.

He reaches in his pocket. "Here's the car for your brother," he says.

The little red Matchbox.

"That's so nice of you, Mike, thanks."

"Make sure you let him think it was Santa, okay?"

"Or the tooth fairy," I say, and we laugh.

I wish all the little ones could meet Mike. They would like him for sure.

We get in the luncheon line. Mike hands me a plate

and we serve ourselves macaroni salad and baked beans. Mike uses silver tongs to put a roll on my plate and one on his and a man in a white jacket and chef's hat serves us each a hamburger.

Maizey waves us to come join her. Billy Hopewell is at the table, too. By the look on Maizey face, I can tell she's got a crush on him. It's amazing how you can know a boy for years and then one day it's like he just moved into town.

Billy and Mike start talking. They are good friends. They're going to football camp together. I look over and see that Sue-Ellen has Eddie Downes right by her side.

"Maize, come get some sodas with me," I say. "Mike, what kind do you like?"

"Orange," he says.

"Me, too," I say. "That's my favorite."

"What kind do you want, Billy?" Maizey asks.

"Cola, please," he says.

"That's my favorite, too," Maizey says in a gushy voice like this is a rare coincidence.

"Come on," I say, grabbing her hand.

By the soda cooler, I tell Maizey about my

Dreamsleeves idea. How she should try it with Billy Hopewell. "But where would I get a sticker?" she says. "And besides, it would be embarrassing if he saw it."

"Let me think," I say. I look around. There's a stack of napkins that say HAPPY BIRTHDAY. I rip off the letter B. "B for Bill," I say. "Here, put this in your pocket."

Maizey laughs. "You're funny, A. You're different. You've changed somehow." She looks in my eyes.

"I've grown up a lot this summer," I say. "A lot happened."

"I'm sorry I haven't called or come over," Maizey says. "I just . . ."

"That's okay," I say.

"No, it's not," Maize says. "And I miss you. Sue-Ellen's fun to hang out with, but she can be stupid as a soap bubble sometimes, and I don't like some of the things she does, like smoking and stuff."

"Come over for lunch tomorrow," I say. "I'll make grilled cheese."

"You and your grilled cheese," Maize says, laughing. "K. Sounds good."

After lunch Mrs. Dandridge processes out slowly, carrying a three-tiered, elaborately frosted birthday cake that I'm certain she did not bake herself, her face glowing in the reflection of the candles, and we all sing.

When Sue-Ellen sits down in what looks like a throne-chair to begin opening her towering tableful of presents, I say, "Uh-oh, this may take a while."

"Wanna go for a walk?" Mike says.

"Sure."

We head away from the pool area and along a paved pathway bordered by perfectly groomed flower beds, not a weed in sight. Nana would be impressed. The golf course is on one side of us, a lake on the other. The path veers up a hill. It is woodsier here, pine trees and oaks. Still not a willow, though. I was sure there would be a willow.

We walk farther. I stumble on an overgrown root. Mike grabs my arm so I won't fall. "Thanks," I say.

"Sure," he says. He takes my hand.

We're holding hands.

Oh my gosh, *we're holding hands*.

We come up on a clearing and there it is.

The giant willow tree.

A breeze blows and the swooping reeds dance, beckoning us over.

"Want to check out that tree?" I say.

"Sure," he says.

Then it's all just like a dream come true. I part the willow's long green rustly braids and we enter, Mike by my side, still holding my hand. The curtains close around us, our own secret garden, and he doesn't waste a moment before he kisses me.

Just a second and then it's over.

I open my eyes and he smiles at me. I smile back.

"Want to get some cake?" he says, sounding a bit relieved.

"You bet," I say, "I'll race you."

Later, Maizey motions to me. We meet in the bathroom.

"I kissed Billy," she whisper-shouts in my ear. "And it was fun! Your dream-thing worked, A!"

"And I kissed Mike," I say. "What a day!"

We link arms and laugh. Maizey hugs me.

I look at the clock, wishing I could stop time, wishing this afternoon could go on forever.

"Two dares down, one to go," Maizey says. She pulls two empty beer cans out of her beach bag.

"Where'd you get those?" I say.

"The garbage," she says.

"What are you going to do with them?"

"We're going to make Sue-Ellen think we did the third dare."

"I don't care what she thinks," I say.

"But what if she says we can't be in her group?"

"Well, then we'll start our own group," I say.

"What kind of group will that be?" Maizey says.

"The no smoking, no drinking, good kissers group."

I manage to sneak back in the house without my father knowing.

"There's a letter for you," Mom says.

Nana. Finally, a letter just for me. She says the baby is adorable, but cranky. She rode on a cable car! She hopes I'm taking care of her garden, weeding and watering. She'll be home a week early. Bitsy's "got the hang of it." In the meantime, she says "buy a treat" with the ten dollars enclosed.

She doesn't say she misses me. Nana's never mushy like that, but she does sign it "Love, Nana."

Ten dollars? Wow! I could buy a jelly donut every day for the whole rest of the year . . . or a peasant blouse . . .

or a new Nancy Drew . . . or maybe go bowling with Mike . . . maybe we could even double date with Maizey and Billy!

> *Dear Diary,*
>
> *Life is good. Dreams come true. I am in love.*
>
> *A*

CHAPTER THIRTY-TWO
Teaching How to Dream

. . . I will wear my heart upon my sleeve.
— SHAKESPEARE

I wish I could write that my mom got my dad to an Alcoholics Anonymous meeting and he stopped drinking and losing his temper and being so strict and that he let me out of jail more and became nice as that father on *The Brady Bunch* and that my mother finished writing her GANE and got it published and it was such a hit that we became millionaires and finally bought our house with the stream and the apple trees.

But in the weeks that followed the pool party, Dad's drinking only got worse and worse until that hot August afternoon, the day we were supposed to leave for our vacation at Uncle Tommy and Aunt Flo's camp, our suitcases all packed and ready to go as soon as

Mom got home from work, when I brought my class down from the school shed at lunchtime, I found my father collapsed on the bathroom floor, in a pool of blood.

"Call . . . an . . . ambulance," he managed to say.

My father's stomach was so damaged from all the drinking and next-day vomiting that he had to have a mesh lining sewn inside him to keep his stomach together. I was in the hallway outside my dad's hospital bed when I heard the doctor tell my mother, "If he keeps drinking, he'll kill himself."

I wish I could write that my father followed his doctor's orders for good, but even though my dad is going to AA meetings and this has been the longest rainbow-stretch in my home that I can ever remember, I've been too fooled by rainbows, however bright, to set my hopes too high. Mom and I are going to Al-Anon meetings and that is good.

We buried Frisky up behind the swing set.

Beck found him all shriveled up under the couch and brought him to me. "I'm sorry, A," he said. Callie cried. We all cried.

I made a little coffin out of an empty matchsticks box, and we gave Frisky a proper funeral. We marched up the hill with a garden shovel, put him to rest, said three prayers, and sang "Let It Be."

"You were a good and loyal pet, Frisky O'Neill," I said. "May you rest in peace."

Maria Carroll calls to see how I'm doing. I tell her things are looking promising. She tells me she can't stop thinking about my wearing that label in church that day so that Father Reilly would see. "That was such a good idea," she says.

"I call it Dreamsleeves," I say.

"Dreamsleeves?" she says. "How perfect. I tried it out with Leo for our anniversary last week and sure enough he just brought me home the sweetest little dog even though he said he didn't want a dog till we got a bigger lot. I've been wanting a dog as long as we've been married, but something about putting that dream on a label — with lots of hearts and *I love you, Leo* written on it — made it come true. Thanks so much for that idea, A. I think you're onto something there. Something really really big."

"Thanks, Maria," I say.

"No, thank *you*, A," she says. "Dreamsleeves. I love it. You should teach people about it."

Up in my Peely-Stick Shop, I lean back on the pine needles and close my eyes. I picture church. Me standing at the pulpit where Father Reilly usually stands. I am talking and the people are listening.

You should teach people about it, Maria said.

Maybe we're all born with one important thing to teach.

Maybe Dreamsleeves is my one thing.

I sit up, excited. I have an idea.

I run down the hill to my room and dig out the ten-dollar bill Nana sent. "May I take the bus up to Woolworth's?" I ask Mom.

She hestitates. I've never been allowed to take the bus uptown by myself before.

"Well, you'll be taking that bus every day to high school in a year, so sure, go ahead. You're old enough."

I kiss my mom and hurry off to go shopping, my heart full of hope.

On Sunday morning I sit at my desk and make out a dream tag and put it in my pocket. I grab the bag from Woolworth's.

At church, I approach the altar, make the sign of the

cross, and then walk into the sacristy. I have never been in here before. It smells like incense and starch.

Father Reilly and the altar boys are getting things ready.

"Excuse me, Father, but can I make an announcement at the end of Mass?"

The priest stares at me for a moment, considering my request.

I want to say "it's the least you can do after you ate all our cake and got me in trouble and didn't help matters out, not one bit," but I just stare at him, squinting my eyes, chin up like my nana does when she means business.

"Okay, Aislinn," he says, "but make it brief, please."

"Sure, Father, no problem. I only have one thing."

When the time is right, Father Reilly nods at me.

I stick my dream on my sleeve and go.

Crossing the white marble altar, I stand at the podium as tall as I can make myself and pull the microphone down closer to my mouth. My feet are cold. My hands are trembling. Seeing all those people staring up at me, I feel light-headed and woozy. I open my mouth, but no words come out. I gulp.

Father Reilly clears his throat like, "it's okay, go ahead."

I search out my mother's face. Our eyes lock. I am okay. She believes in me.

"My name is Aislinn, old Irish for 'dream.' I want to be a teacher someday. I think maybe every person comes born with one important thing to teach. This is mine.

"If you have a dream, you should wear it on your sleeve, right out where everyone can see it. I call this idea Dreamsleeves.

"I think it's wrong to keep our dreams hidden. We write them in diaries or on slips of paper in a box where no one else can see.

"We need other people to help make our dreams come true.

"But how can people help if they don't know what we want?

"Just think if maybe the person you shook hands with during the Sign of Peace, or the person you'll pass in the parking lot, or a friend you've known for years but haven't shared your secret with" — I search and find Maria Carroll's face — "who knows but maybe that person might be the exact perfect one who can help you make your wish come true.

"Imagine if your dream was right on your sleeve. It would be so easy then, right?"

The church is silent. You aren't supposed to talk.

"I will be at the back of church today with dream-tag labels for anyone who wants one. They are free, my gift to you. You can get more at Woolworth's."

My body's rumbling like Niagara Falls. I wobbly-walk across the altar and down the steps, pausing to bow my head before returning to my seat.

B, C, and D clap for me.

Mom runs her finger across the words on my sleeve. *Teach How to Dream.*

"You do, A," she says, "you do."

Tears are rolling down my father's face.

He looks at me, really looks at me, and I smile, really smile at him.

The old man in the brown suit with the seagull feather in his hat is the first one in line for a label. Many others follow.

Maria Carroll swoops me up in a hug. "I'm so proud of you I could scream!"

When we get home from church, I stay back as my family heads up the side of the house. I kneel down, wipe the dirt from that one basement window, and look in.

There's the bar I sat propped on the night I was a princess.

I stand and turn and run.

I run down the front steps, down the street to the concrete wall by the bridge. I slip through the opening, I knew I could, down a pathway someone made through the weeds, I wonder who cleared this, across the asphalt pavement, traffic rumbling by on the bridge high above me, across the railroad tracks, more pavement, weeds, rushes, and rocks, and then I'm right by it.

The river.

I squat down, lean over, and stick my hand in the water.

CHAPTER THIRTY-THREE
Free

And whatever your labors and aspirations,
in the noisy confusion of life keep peace with your soul.
With all its sham, drudgery and broken dreams,
it is still a beautiful world.
— MAX EHRMANN

Nana comes home. We keep our tradition. I buy loafers you can stick pennies in. While we're waiting for our tuna fish sandwiches in our booth at Manory's, I tell her about Dreamsleeves, just the idea, I don't tell her about standing up and talking from the pulpit. She'd probably say that was too bold, sacrilegious even, and then say, "I hope you were wearing a hat at least."

I don't tell Nana, but I bet I get my courage from her. You must have to be pretty bold to be the first ever woman leader of the workers' union.

"I was wondering how you were spending your time," Nana says. "My flowers looked like they haven't seen a hose in weeks."

"Oh, Nana, come on. I watered them. They just missed you. Everybody knows you're the real gardener in the family."

On the day of the Town Picnic, I help my mom pack sandwiches and salads and sodas and we all go to Frear Park for the day.

Beck takes his bat and ball. Dooley's got his cars.

"Bring your guitar, A," Callie says. I pack some bubbles, too.

Dad takes Mom's arm to walk her down to the car. Her belly's as big as a mountain now.

The park is filled with families at tables and on blankets with picnic baskets and coolers, radios playing, smoke rising from grills, a badminton game, volleyball, college kids tossing a Frisbee. Up on the hill, there's a boy trying to fly a kite. Two little girls, Callie's age, run out from under the sprinklers holding hands, giggling, dripping wet.

"Let's try to find a spot in the shade," Mom says.

Maria Carroll stands and waves to us from inside the

pavilion. "Aislinn!" she calls, "Maggie! Over here. We've got room."

When I reach Maria, she points toward the next picnic table over. "Look!"

It's the old man from church in his brown suit and feathered hat who was first in line for a Dreamsleeve label.

He sees me and stands, comes to shake my hand. "I'm Patrick Leary," he says. "I was a friend of your grandfather's. He was a good man."

Mr. Leary touches his Dreamsleeve. It reads *Meet my grandchildren.*

The two little girls I saw giggling out under the sprinklers come running in and pull on his leg. "Come on, Grandpa. Come watch us!"

He looks at me with tears in his eyes. "You gave me the courage," he says.

"For what?" I say.

"To tell my daughter I was sorry and get my family back again."

"And look, A," Maria says, pulling my arm. "There's another person wearing a label over there, and look, two tables back, see?"

People wearing dreams on their sleeves. I can't wait to read them.

A cry catches in my throat. I gulp. My eyes fill with tears.

Maria hugs me. "You started something good here, A. I knew it was a big idea."

My family comes up behind us. Maria shows them what we're looking at.

"I told you Dreamsleeves was catchy," Mom says.

"We tried it first," Callie brags.

"No . . . you were second," Beck says.

"O . . . *kay*," Callie says, rolling her eyes.

"I got my red car with it," Dooley says.

From Santa Mike. I smile, wishing he was here.

"*Dreamsleeves*, you call it, right?" a lady standing by us says.

"It's my daughter's idea," Dad says, nodding proudly. "That's my daughter."

It was a nice nearly-end-of-summer day.

Mike wasn't at the park, but I'll see him soon enough.

School starts next week.

Hopefully, this is also the start of happier days for me and my family, filled with rainbows and pots of gold and that house with the apple trees.

And no more drinking, no more tempers, no more being scared.

I learned a lot this summer. I know I cannot control any of that.

What I do know is this:

I know how to dream.

And because of that,

I, Aislinn, aka "Dream" O'Neill,

will always and forever be

free.

MAKE YOUR OWN DREAM TAGS

If you'd like to try Dreamsleeves, peel-off labels work nicely, or here are a few slips you can copy, cut out, and attach. Good luck and happy dreaming!

My dream is:

My dream is:

My dream is:

ACKNOWLEDGMENTS

With thanks, first and foremost, to my mother, Peg Spain Murtagh, who always makes me feel like I can accomplish every dream I dream.

To my brother, Jerry Murtagh, whose face lit with excitement when I told him about the Dreamsleeves idea. Such enthusiasm is a rare and priceless gift.

To my sister, Noreen Mahoney, who listened to all my fledging stories back when I was desperately trying to get published and who somehow always found a way to be encouraging. Thank you for believing in me, Nor.

To my agent, Tracey Adams, who knew I was ready to write this book, and supported me every step of the way.

To my editor, Jennifer Rees, who loved the idea from the start and then challenged me to take it further. Your mark is on this one, Jen. And to David Levithan and Elizabeth Parisi and all of the fabulously talented people at Scholastic Press, Scholastic Book Clubs, and Book Fairs.

To my seventh-grade friends Joan Garbowski, Marie Hogan, Christine Casey, Mary Madden, Theresa Maloney, Joanne Fin, and Mary Hennessy.

To fellow writer and kindred spirit Sara Webb Quest for a particularly nourishing conversation about this story as we walked "the Spit" on Popponesset Beach, Cape Cod.

Always and forever to my beautiful, smart, and huge-hearted sons Dylan, Connor, and Christopher Murtagh Paratore. You are this mother's dream come true.

And to you, my loyal readers. May you close this book inspired to open something new and wonderful in your life.

Dream Big.
If you can dream it, you can do it,
wear it on your sleeve and believe.
I'll be rooting for you!!
Coleen ☺